ZOLI'S LEGACY
BOOK II: BEQUEST

DAWN L. WATKINS

Library of Congress Cataloging-in-Publication Data:

Watkins, Dawn L.
  Zoli's legacy / Dawn L. Watkins.

      Contents: bk. 1. Inheritance—bk. 2. Bequest
      Summary: Zoli, a student in Hungary between the world wars,
  struggles for his education against poverty, his father's displeasure,
  and his own pride. As Hungary is drawn into the conflict of World
  War II, Zoli takes charge of an orphanage, marries, and becomes a
  soldier and father.
      ISBN 0-89084-596-4 (v. 1)—ISBN 0-89084-597-2 (v. 2)
      1. Hungary—History—1918-1945—Juvenile fiction.   [1. Hun-
  gary—History—1918-1945—Fiction.   2. Christian life—Fiction.]
  I. Title.
  PZ7.W268Zo   1991
  [Fic]—dc20   91-29300
                                                                      CIP
                                                                       AC

Zoli's Legacy
Book II: Bequest

Dawn L. Watkins

Edited by Carolyn Cooper and Rebecca S. Moore

©1991 Bob Jones University Press
Greenville, South Carolina 29614

ISBN 0-89084-597-2

20   19   18   17   16   15   14   13   12   11   10   9   8   7

Acknowledgments
Special thanks to Peter Gaal for interviews and tapes,
and to Lisa Gaal and Molly Bulla
for careful and patient transcription.

CZECHO-
SLOVAKIA

RUMANIA

Hungary today
Part of Hungary before
the Treaty of Trianon

Publisher's Note

The two volumes of *Zoli's Legacy* follow Zoltán Galambos through thirty years of Hungarian history, marking his choices and revealing their outcomes. Although the times around him are unsettled–from World War I until just after World War II–Zoli has a legacy that sustains him and that throughout proves larger than any circumstances.

The background of *Book II: Bequest* is Europe under the growing threat of Adolph Hitler. Regent Horthy had managed to regain the land Hungary lost in the Treaty of Trianon without compromising himself or his country. His government attempted for several years to maintain Hungary's independence, to resist the Germans, and to avoid Nazi occupation. Horthy foresaw the great war and believed that Germany would almost surely lose in the end to the sea powers.

When Germany annexed Czechoslovakia, the part of Hungary that had been under Czech rule came back to Hungarian hands, as did other lands a year later. Until 1944, Horthy's government maneuvered skillfully around Hitler. The country became a haven for Jews, accepting those fleeing from Rumania, Germany, and Poland. Later, the Hungarian government passed mild anti-Jewish legislation to mollify German demands while at the same time protecting the Jewish community as a whole.

After Hungary fell to Germany, an even worse fate awaited the country: liberation by the Russian army. The end of World War II was only the beginning of war for the Magyars. The Russian occupation stripped Hungary of all its national and human rights and laid siege to more than the land. The very spirit of Hungary was at risk.

This second volume of *Zoli's Legacy* concludes the narrative of his salvation and surrender. Now a husband and a father, Zoli makes his decisions knowing that everything he does affects many other people. When Hungary is occupied by German soldiers and then by Russian "liberators," Zoli chooses the daring way out. He leaves behind a far greater legacy than he had thought possible as a boy listening for the train in his home village, years before.

Contents

1937-1947

But seek ye first the kingdom of God,
and his righteousness;
and all these things shall be added unto you.

Matthew 6:33

Chapter One
The Ends of Work

1937

Mrs. Toth gazed at me through the screen door of the orphanage.

"Yes?"

"Mrs. Toth, I'm Zoltán Galambos. I think I—"

"Zoltán! I didn't know you. How you've changed! Come in. Please! Bring in your things!"

She swung open the door of the orphanage.

"My husband will be so happy to see you here already."

I set my books down by the threshold. I stepped inside the building that still smelled of fresh-cut lumber. Some of the windowsills were planed smooth but were yet unvarnished. The whole was airy and clean, and it occurred to me that I had always lived in old buildings. It made me think of Milike and her vision of America as a fresh and untrammeled place.

Mrs. Toth leaned slightly left and looked past me to the porch and then back at me.

I smiled as a man might who is out of practice with smiling. I set down my parcel of books.

"My baggage is all in."

She tilted her head.

"Oh. Well, come along and let me find my husband. He has a thousand things lined up for you. I hope you came with a will to work."

"Yes," I said. And little else, I thought.

"Zoltán!" The booming voice caught me just as a big hand closed over mine. He shook it vigorously, as he had that day Bootblack and I had come to him by the soccer field in Farna.

"You've come early."

He looked me up and down, and I felt the statement was a cloaked question.

"Is that all right? I shouldn't want to—"

"All right? It's an answer to prayer, young man."

Mrs. Toth said, "Let's show him to his quarters first." She leaned sideways toward me. "Once he gets to talking about the orphanage, you'll never get settled."

"Sure," said Toth. "Where are your things? I'll help you carry them up."

"I've only some books in the hall," I said. "I can get them."

"Get them then," he said. "Let's be going."

The room was well swept and spacious. The light came in through the windows in broad bands and laid bright squares on the floor.

"I meant to have some more things ready for you," said Mrs. Toth.

She pulled open the drawers of a bureau.

"Will this be room enough? If you—"

She stopped and her lower lip pulled in as though she had remembered something important. Toth looked at the books and then at me.

"Zoltán," he said. "This is really all? No other clothes?"

I shook my head.

"Is this something I might ask about?" he said.

Mrs. Toth put her hand out to him, to stop him.

"I brought only what I have bought for myself," I said. "And as you can see, my interests are more in books than in fashion."

Toth looked me up and down. "But you can't wear books, my friend."

"I'll see what might be here that he could use," said Mrs. Toth. She went out with the step women have when they are going with good purpose.

"Here's a desk at any rate," said Toth.

He picked up a few books and put them on the desk.

The bed stood between the door and the windows, without linens. Beside it was a lamp with a cord running down to the floor and then along the wall and up to a plug in the wall by the door.

"Electricity," I said.

"Well," said Toth, "I had the wires put in, but we don't have the electricity."

"Do you live here?"

"We do. But now that you're here, we can be going to Farna. I have work there too, and my wife has her mother to look after."

"Oh. Right away?"

"Not to worry," he said. "I'll be coming every few weeks."

"Where are the orph–boys?" I said.

"At school."

"The Gymnásium is still in?"

"Yes."

It seemed to me that time and the seasons were out of motion somehow, as though I had gotten lost in the turning of clock hands and calendar pages.

Mrs. Toth returned with an armload of clothes.

"These are some trousers that someone–" She looked over at Toth and nodded at his girth. "–can no longer wear. I brought them in case some fellow could use them."

She handed me a pair.

"Try these on, and I'll go get my pins. I can make a few adjustments in them quick as a wink."

I did as I was told, and when she knocked, both her husband and I said, "Come in."

She swept in, her sewing basket on her arm and pins already sticking out of her mouth. She stopped short at the door.

I held the trousers up in great handfuls above my waist, the wide legs gathering like sails to skinny masts and ending in piles of fabric over my shoes. I must have looked to her like a badly made mop.

She put her hand to her mouth.

"What do you think?" said Toth. "Can they be fixed?"

She slowly shook her head.

"Well," he said, turning to me, "don't lose weight."

And Mrs. Toth was free at last to laugh.

We went into Komárom, and Mrs. Toth bought me a brand-new suit. I asked her whom I could pay back when I got the money, but she only waved her hand at me.

"The Lord provided," she said.

When the boys came from school that day, they had a new headmaster, all turned out in neat suit pants and a clean shirt.

Thirty boys, some as tall as I, rushed past me toward the upstairs. They threw down their schoolbooks by the stairs, yelling to each other and banging into each other.

"They're all yours," said Toth.

They went by again by pairs and groups, in old clothes, and out to the field to play soccer. For two hours or more they ran after the ball and each other.

By and by, they came toward the building again, slower now, but just as loud.

The kitchen vibrated with their shouts. Two women hurried to put down kettles on the table and lay out trays of bread. The boys plunged the dippers into the kettles and sloshed the stew into their bowls. The bread disappeared like snow in the April sun.

One woman carried away a tray and refilled it, and the other went down the tables filling the glasses with milk. The woman with the tray came back, little beads of sweat shining in her hairline. She looked dark under her eyes, and older than her blond hair seemed to indicate.

For a while, the shouting died into a slurping and jostling, and then it swelled again. The boys skidded back their benches. The spoons clanged into empty bowls and a few rattled onto the floor. The boys left in groups, twos and threes and fours, and thundered up the stairs. I could hear them overhead, running and shouting.

The women began to take up the bowls and the glasses. I stood in the doorway, still expecting to find a reason for what had just gone on.

"Excuse me."

The women looked up.

"I'm Zoltán Galambos. I think I'm to be in charge here."

"Hello," said the older woman. "Everyone calls me Kis néni. I'm always the nanny."

The blonde said nothing. Kis néni tucked a loose pin back into her knot of white hair.

"You are the cook?" I asked.

She laughed. "And everything."

"I see."

"This is Greta. From Germany."

"My husband was Hungarian," she said. It was a thready voice, whether from habit or exhaustion I could not tell.

I nodded. They seemed to be unsure whether to go on with the work or wait for me to say more.

"Let me help you," I said.

Kis néni nodded once and handed me a cloth. She had big hands that were knobbed at the joints and chapped.

I scraped a plate onto another.

"Is it always so?" I asked.

"Yes," said Greta. "They run wild like pigs."

From the window I could see the boys playing soccer again, and some of the smaller ones wrestling on the sidelines.

"You are young," said Kis néni.

"That may come in handy," I said.

*   *   *

In the morning, before light, I heard tables being moved in the kitchen. I dressed quickly and went down. Kis néni and Greta were already laying out plates for breakfast.

"You're here early," I said.

Kis néni yawned and patted her mouth. She stood beside a lantern hanging by the wall. It still swung a little, and the shadows wavered back and forth around her.

"Yes," she said. "But much is to be done."

"What can I do to help?"

I tucked in my shirt and rolled up the sleeves.

"You could make sandwiches," said Greta. "The stuff is there." She pointed to a worktable by the sink. "And wrap each one in a paper. Here, I'll show you."

The first light began to come in the windows after perhaps the fifteenth sandwich. Upstairs no one had begun to stir.

"I'll call the boys," said Kis néni, "or do you want to?"

I took from her tone that she preferred that I call them.

I went upstairs and down the hall, throwing doors open as I went and bellowing.

"Up, boys. The day's got the jump on you. Let's go!"

It was the only time I can remember wishing for the blaring bells of the dormitory in Bratislava.

"Who are you?" The voice came from the dim lower bunk in the last room.

"The new headmaster."

"Well, all right, then."

The boy rolled out and stood up.

I went back down the hall.

"Any boy not down in fifteen minutes is out of his breakfast."

Toth arrived amid the charge for the tables. Above the clamor of breakfast, he banged the sink with a metal ladle. All heads turned his way.

"Good morning, fellows."

"Good morning." The response was jumbled and feeble.

"This is Zoltán Galambos. He has come to be the headmaster here."

Thirty pairs of eyes looked me over.

He laughed his hearty laugh, too big for the small hour, I thought.

"Don't think you can slip anything by him, boys. He's an old hand at this."

In a while, the racket rose to its old level.

"I have been walking them to the school. But I expect you know where it is, yes?" said Toth to me.

I nodded and surveyed the company I would have.

The walk was not long, but I could see the wisdom of having a sheep dog herd the sheep toward the Gymnásium. The older boys made a sport of hijacking the younger ones for their sandwiches. And the younger ones had to be prodded to keep going toward their own school.

Shirttails hung out from waistbands at every angle and not one head of hair looked sufficiently combed. But the shoes, I noticed, were all shined.

"Mr. Galambos?"

I looked at the boy beside me.

"Hello."

"You don't remember me, but I used to call you Zoli bacsi. A long time ago, up in Farna."

The face joggled something way back in my mind.

"I'm Dani."

I saw suddenly the same face, smaller and fearful, in the lamplight in the night. And I remembered the little scorekeeper who could not count over ten. I felt a pang at realizing he was still an orphan, still waiting to be wanted.

"Why sure," I said. "I hardly knew you. You're so big. What are you now? Nine?"

"Yes, sir."

He said nothing more, but just as before, he walked beside me, his chin tucked slightly, asking by his posture not to be sent away.

I dispatched the Gymnásium boys to the lane I knew well, the winding path to Latin and history and mathematics. I thought of following them, to see Kovaly. I missed the man, his warmth and steadiness. And yet I remembered too distinctly the last time I had seen him. Though letters had passed between us since, I feared that my behavior then must surely have changed things too much. I chose to remember how it used to be than to know with certainty that the old bond was gone.

A little way on, I said good-bye to the younger fellows. I felt embarrassed at their ragged collars and their thin pants. A few waved to me, and I, but an older version of them, waved back.

At the orphanage, the tables were cleared and the plates stacked at the ready for supper. The kettles hung drying by the back door; the towels aired on the edge of the sink.

Upstairs, Kis néni and Greta were making beds. The hall had been swept as far as the room they were in, the brooms resting against the doorjamb. The two women lifted the mattress together and snapped the sheet under it, and in the same motion, pulled the top of the sheet to the pillow.

Greta saw me out of the corner of her eye.

"What are you doing?"

"Watching," I said. "And learning."

I swept the rest of the hall. When I came back, Greta had moved on to the next room.

The washbasins were dry, the pitchers empty. I lifted the towel on the stand. It was dry as well.

"Kis néni," I said, "has everything been going about as usual around here? Last night and today, I mean?"

She straightened up from thumping a pillow into place.

"Pretty much."

"You always make the beds?"

"Sure."

She stared at me for a moment and then went past me and took up her broom. She walked from side to side, so much so that as she went toward the stairs her head and shoulder eclipsed the end window at every other step.

"Let me carry that stuff," I said.

I took her broom and the bed linens from her. She yielded them up without argument and took the rail of the stairs.

"You can just put them in the closet off the kitchen," she said. She motioned, more to let me know I was not to wait for her than to show me the way.

The closet was full of laundry to be done and scrub brushes, worn down nearly to the wood, and buckets. On a shelf by the door was a pile of rags. And stacked beside them were several tins of shoe polish.

I opened a tin, the familiar smell rising from it, and studied the evidence. I snapped the lid on again and went out.

That afternoon when the boys came tearing in from school, I met them at the stairs. I stood three steps up, leaning on the rail.

They halted at the bottom and milled in the lobby. But they did not go out again or ask any questions.

"Good afternoon, gentlemen."

A couple of the smaller boys answered me.

I came down a step.

"I'm glad to see you home."

Still they said nothing.

"I've been just looking around," I said, "seeing how things go around here. And I've noticed a job or two that needs a man, but I haven't the time. I thought I might look over this group here and see if I could find a suitable worker."

"What jobs?" one of the tallest boys said.

"Well, for starters, splitting wood and carrying water."

"Mr. Toth did that," said a boy with wavy black hair.

I ignored the rustle among the troops.

"And shining shoes."

"Ahh," the first boy said.

I sat down on the second stair. "Kis néni does that now, doesn't she? Every night while you sleep. Well. That's no job for women. They haven't got the arm for it. A man can get a real shine on leather when he wants to."

I slid my foot out and leaned back on the third stair. A few eyes went down to my gleaming shoe and back to me.

"But," I said, "maybe there's no one here to do it but me. Thing is, I just have so much else to do."

There was no volunteer, but neither were there any deserters.

"And," I said, "men have to learn to look after themselves. Kis néni and Mrs. Greta won't always be around. What I like is independence. Don't you?"

I waited. At last, Dani spoke up.

"I'll do it, sir."

A bigger boy said, "You? It'll take you a week to learn how."

The tallest of them spoke again. "Can't you idiots see what he's doing? He's tricking you into doing his work."

I stood up slowly and glowered down on him. "No, boy, I'm trying to trick you into doing your own work. But if you won't be coaxed, there are other methods."

* * *

"What is this?"

I held out a pair of pants with a rip in them.

The boy, Feri, stared up at me, as though I were some kind of annoying fly.

"Pants."

I thumbed the tear, holding up the triangle piece.

"You can't wear these to school."

"I guess I can." He glared at me now.

The bed he sat on was not yet made. I felt my impatience come up like mercury in a thermometer.

"Come down and I will show you how to mend these."

"No."

I was astonished. In my whole experience with life, open rebellion to an authority had missed me. I continued to gaze at the boy, thinking surely he would repent and get up. He did not.

"Feri, come with me."

Still he sat there. Other boys had gathered in the hall and were looking in the room.

I shifted my weight back.

"So you want to look like a ragbag? Fine. Let the others laugh at you and say 'Poor orphan.' Go around like that, if you want."

He arched his eyebrow and smirked.

"But in the meantime, you can spend supper time up here."

There was a ripple behind me.

"You can't do that!" the boy said.

"Watch."

I went out and closed the door.

During supper, Feri appeared in the kitchen doorway, looking iike a stray dog. The others glanced in his direction and then at me.

I said, "Isn't this good, boys?"

I laid some butter thickly on my bread.

"You are to be in your room, Feri."

"I'm hungry."

"Have you changed your mind about mending?"

He said nothing.

"Go upstairs."

"You're mean." He threw his shoulder outward as he spoke.

All the eyes came back to me. I put down my knife.

"If I gave you no choice, I would be mean."

"What do you know about it?" he demanded.

"Plenty. Now go."

He stood there, playing with the idea of defying me.

I stood up then, and he fled.

*   *   *

By the end of the next week, there was a new order at the Komárom orphanage. Every boy made his own bed and carried his own plate to the sink after meals. The shining of shoes and the splitting of wood were rotated among the privileged older few. Younger boys watched as though from the sidelines of a soccer game and begged for something important to do.

"Please, Zoli bacsi," they said, "you can trust us. We'll do a good job."

"Well, I don't know," I said. I rubbed the back of my neck. "This sweeping is tricky. It's not as simple as it looks."

"Show us how," they said.

I drew my hand across my chin as if in deep thought. "I guess we could try it for a week. See how it goes. But if it starts to look shabby in here, I'll have to take the job back myself."

I did not have to take the job back. I made a large paper wheel with all the sweeping, dusting, table setting, dish washing, and water carrying chores on it. On a smaller wheel, I put all the boys' names. I fixed one wheel over the other, and each week I turned the names so that every boy had a new job. I found this method prevented boredom and quarreling and gave experience to all.

Greta did the laundry and mending, and Kis néni did the cooking. I put myself to the hard work of the orphanage–getting money to support the place and teaching the boys how to get along in the life that stretched before them.

I also had a moment then to write to Milike, to tell her all that had transpired since I had left Bratislava, and to ask her–and Pali–to visit me in my new home. I posted the letter with some anxiousness and stewed over it for three days, until I was certain it could not but be in her hands, and then I asked God to give me patience and plunged wholeheartedly back into the work before me.

Every night after supper, I read to the boys from the Bible. At first I chose verses from the Proverbs about the value of hard work and obedience. I watched the faces, some smooth with innocence, some already cloudy with bitterness and rebellion. The tallest boy, Gab, had eyes like stones. His chin jutted out in constant defiance of all the world.

"Now," I said, closing the Bible, "I think we should talk about homework. I haven't seen any being done around here. Surely you all have some."

"No," said Gab, "they don't give orphans homework because they don't have homes to work it in."

He meant to anger me, but all he gave me was a vision of myself apart from the grace of God and the hand of Kovaly.

The boys looked to me with wide eyes, expecting perhaps a sermon or punishment for Gab. Gab's chair balanced on the two back legs.

"Boys," I said, "when your parents died, God gave you many mothers and fathers in their stead. You have Mrs. Greta and Kis néni and Pastor Toth and me. And as your Papa, I'm asking you, where is your homework?"

Gab's chair slammed down. "You are not my father!"

"Suit yourself. But where is your homework?"

His eyes blazed at me.

"Get your notebook," I said.

Still he sat there with his fiery look, his chest going up and down as though he had been running.

"Get it or I go with you to the Gymnásium tomorrow."

The other boys looked at him cautiously. He finally stood and cast his chair backward and strode out. The others looked again to me, waiting.

"From now on," I said, "you will do your homework and show it to me."

The eyes went down to the tables and plates.

"You have to learn to work. Knowing how to work makes you enjoy your life. Don't you want the pleasure of being able to do many kinds of things?"

"Yes." The replies put all together made but a feeble response.

Gab returned and threw the notebook down in front of me so that it spun to a stop just beside my hand.

"Very good. Now I'm going to put a note to the teacher here, asking him to write the assignment out so that I can check on it."

Kis néni smiled over from her chair by the stove and nodded.

"And before you do any chores tonight, I want to see everyone's notebook. And if you don't have a notebook, we'll send a piece of paper to your teacher."

I gave Gab his book, looking at him directly.

"The rest of you can go," I said. "Bring me your notebooks."

They piled out of the kitchen. I had not taken my eyes from Gab.

"Gab, the handwriting in this book is terrible. Now, I know you can do better. I suspect you are the smartest boy in your class. Why do you make an effort to hide it?"

"You think you know all about it, don't you?"

"More than you think."

"What do you care about my handwriting?"

"I care about your handwriting because I care about you. If you have the right heart, you'll have a better hand. Laziness has many witnesses."

"You're not fooling me," he said.

"I'm not trying to. And you're not fooling me."

He shoved away from the wall he had been leaning on and, looking at me as he might at a growling dog, went out.

Kis néni said, "You're not as young as you look."

* * *

I took the office of treasurer in the local Reformed church. Each day, after I walked the boys to school, I went to the church until one o'clock. I kept the books, collected and counted donations and the church taxes. But I always made it a point to be at the orphanage when the boys came in.

The last week of school came slow enough for the boys and too soon for me. I went down the hall on the last day.

"Come on, get up, boys."

There were mumbled replies mostly, and an occasional "coming." Dani came out to meet me.

I stopped at one door, as usual, to be sure I was obeyed.

"Gab, the ladies are depending on you. Is there wood in?"

"I guess."

"Not good enough, Gab. Where's your sense of honor?"

"My what?"

I sighed. "No wood, no food. Choose."

When I came back from the far room, Dani was sitting on the steps.

"Zoli bacsi," said Dani, "why do you have two jobs?"

"Oh, I have something I want to buy."

"Do you have to buy it yourself?"

"Yes."

"Are you an orphan?"

The question went through me like an arrow. I sat down on the stairs beside him. In all the business of the past two weeks, I had not had time to feel that old pain.

"In a way," I said. "But people as old as I am are their own parents."

"Oh. I'd rather have someone else besides me, though," he said.

I patted his head. "You do, remember?"

He grinned at me, like the little Dani of Farna.

"What will we do when school is out?"

"I think I will have to hold some summer school," I said. "Most of the grades are pretty bad around here."

Dani nodded.

"I'm sorry, Zoli bacsi. I don't learn very fast."

"You'll get it," I said. "Wanting to is most of the job. And I think we might farm a little. Grow vegetables and maybe get a cow or two. What do you think?"

His eyes brightened with the thought. It seemed I could see a farmer behind those eyes. And I felt my own pulse quicken to imagine a huge garden behind the kitchen.

Greta appeared in the doorway between the kitchen and the main hall. Her face was white, her eyes wide. I stood up.

"Zoltán," she said, barely a whisper, "Kis néni died last night."

Chapter Two
Investments

The church filled with the friends of Kis néni. The casket sat open at the front of the altar, and from where I sat, the white hair and the pillow under it blended into a light around the old head that had rest now forever. Her hands were folded over her, and the gnarled joints were no longer red with pain.

Toth preached the funeral. He spoke more quietly than I had ever heard him in the pulpit, as though Kis néni might be awakened. Dani sat with me. He had made no room for discussion; he had just walked in on my right, and like a shadow, stayed with me.

"She spent her life in the service of others," Toth was saying. "A true example of the believer. This last year she gave herself to the orphanage, and perhaps it was her greatest gift, to put the love and time she had left into the lives of so many boys."

I had known her little more than two weeks, and yet I felt the truth of his words, as tangibly as I felt the hand that stole into mine and held on. Dani did not look up at me, but the grasp on my right hand told me everything.

Greta sat near the front, dressed in black. She did not move at all. Beside her was Mrs. Toth, whose hand went again and again to her eyes. I glanced at the boys lined up in the pews ahead of me. Their stillness astonished me, and pleased me.

We sang a hymn. Toth closed the lid of the casket. And then the pallbearers, eight men, young and old, among them Gab, who had asked for the honor, picked up their burden and went out. We followed behind into the graveyard by the church where the morning shone on the shoulders of the bearers, a morning frail compared to the one Kis néni woke to.

At the orphanage, there was little talking. Gab sat on the porch looking toward the church. The stiffness had gone out of his shoulders. He did not lean against the post, but rather into himself.

In the afternoon a few of the younger boys went out to get up a game of soccer. I would have made no move to stop them, but Dani ran out to them and threw himself on the biggest of them, swinging his fists and yelling.

"Here," I said, "here. Dani!"

I wrestled him off the other boy, who, taken totally unawares, was flat on the ground.

"Dani, listen to me. Stop!"

I held him away and looked at him. His eyes welled, and he tried to pull back. Still I held him.

"Don't let them play. Don't let them!"

"All right," I said. "All right."

I turned to the others, who stood silent and watchful. I motioned with my head that they should go elsewhere. They went, without arguing, in different directions.

A sob broke from the boy in my hands, from the center of him, as though it would shake him in two. I let him go and opened my arms. He came into them and wept, for Kis néni, for himself, for, I imagined, many losses never recognized.

* * *

"You're not a very good cook," said Gab.

"This is true," I said.

The boys laughed.

"Why can't Mrs. Greta cook?" said one boy. "Or Mrs. Toth?"

"Mrs. Greta has enough to do keeping your clothes clean. And Pastor Toth told you he and his wife had to go home."

"Will we starve?" asked another.

"Pastor Toth says he has asked a cook from another orphanage to come to our rescue," I said.

"I hope it's Mrs. Vrabel," said Dani. "She's the best cook I ever saw."

The others looked at him, surprised because he rarely spoke at meals and also because he was not usually so definite in his opinions.

Dani looked over at me and smiled as people who share ground smile at each other. Many of the boys had come down from Farna, but only Dani was left from the summer of Mrs. Vrabel.

I remembered the cooking, and the daughters.

"And she made you eat what she cooked, too, I recall," I said.

Dani's face turned red. I could still see him being toted back to the table like a sack on the woman's hip.

It had never occurred to me that Toth might get Mrs. Vrabel.

School was out, officially, but still in at the orphanage, unofficially. I held summer school in the afternoons to ready the boys for the next year of school. We studied Latin and mathematics and even English.

"And everyone who can't write neatly will write it again," I said.

The group groaned a little.

"Here are your papers from yesterday."

Gab was nearly the last to come for his paper.

"You are doing much better," I said. "I knew you could."

He grabbed the paper away, but he smiled as he turned away with it.

"All right," I said, closing my books and stacking them, "who wants to play soccer?"

Every morning I gave out the assignments before I left for my work at the church. They were never as hard or as long as any given out in regular school, but the season made them seem so to the students.

Dani said, "Why don't you tell us our assignments after class in the afternoons?"

"Well," I said, "three reasons. One, I don't always have them ready."

This answer seemed to surprise, and gratify, several boys.

"Two, you might forget by the next day anyway. And three–"

They were all listening now.

"I don't want to ruin a good soccer game by hanging school-work over it."

Dani grinned.

"Now you all have your chores and your assignments. All right? And when you are done," I said, "ask Gab to check your work. When I get home, I'll teach you the next lesson."

The word *home* had a good sound to it, in that sentence, to those of us who were yet struggling toward a satisfactory definition. Gab looked up and stared at me.

"And then we'll play soccer?" said the one with the wavy hair.

"'Til the sun sets," I said.

I got my fourth pay from the church. I laid the forints on the desk and drew the rest of my money out of my pocket. I counted it, as though I did not know exactly how much was there. I left a little early that day and went shopping in Komárom.

The woman brought out a bolt of cloth for me and opened a length of it.

"Good material," she said. "See how you can't see my hand through it?"

"How much of it do you have?"

"Two bolts like this one," she said.

"Would that be enough to make thirty boys' shirts?"

"Thirty–are you from the new orphanage?"

I nodded.

She tilted her head and squinted her eyes. "Yes, it might be a little more than you need. Since it's for the boys, I'll tell you what. Bring back what you don't use, and I'll give back that much money."

"Thank you," I said. "That's good of you. How much do I owe?"

"Well, let's see. Thirty-five forints."

I laid out the bills. As she counted them, I noticed a machine in the corner by the window, not exactly a sewing machine and not exactly a knitting machine.

"What is that?"

She glanced over. "Oh, that. It's a sock machine. You know, that knits socks. Someone put it in here to try to sell it, but like I told him, nobody around here can afford such a contraption. Especially when anybody can knit a pair of socks."

"How much is it?"

She laughed. "Seven hundred forints."

I went back toward the orphanage with two bolts of cloth under my arm and five forints in my pocket. Now I had only to convince Greta that this was a good idea. I did not know whether she could make thirty shirts by the fall.

Several boys were waiting on the porch for me. They pounced on me with the news.

"She's here. The new cook. It's the one Dani wanted."

"So soon?"

"Just in time," said Gab. "It's still early enough for her to make supper."

"What's that you've got?" one asked.

"Something for Mrs. Greta," I said.

Mrs. Vrabel had the stove going and the boys running for water, wood, and potatoes. Her bags were still sitting just inside the door between the kitchen and the hall.

"Mrs. Vrabel," I said. "Thank you for coming."

She turned from the stove and surveyed me. "Zoltán Galambos."

She pronounced my name so as to summarize all past history and all present circumstances at once.

She looked exactly the same, tall, forceful, completely able. And her step was the same, I saw, when she went to the sink.

"Any of these boys know how to peel potatoes?" she said.

I motioned to Dani and two others standing by. They got out paring knives and immediately set to peeling. I could not tell whether it was Mrs. Vrabel's manner or the week and a half of eating my cooking that made them so compliant.

"Would you like me to take your things to your room?" I said.

She glanced over. "No," she said, "that can wait. Supper's at five."

* * *

As an officer of the church, I was allowed to attend board meetings. I was also there to see to the interests of the orphanage. I had had a plan for some time that I was waiting to find an opening to present.

"All right," said Toth. "That's the old business. What new business?"

Before I could speak, an older man cleared his throat.

"As you all know," he said, "I run a little bookstore, and the proceeds go to the orphanage."

"No," I said, "I didn't know."

Heads turned to me.

Toth said, "Kalocsai here sells Christian books from a little shop in town. He donates his time, as he has another job. And any proceeds go to the orphanage fund."

I nodded.

"Anyway," the man continued, "I am running into a little trouble. Since I opened the store, I learned that I have to get a permit."

We all waited to see what the trouble was.

He turned his hat around in his hands. "Well," he said, "I can't have the permit because they say I do not have enough education to run a bookstore."

The silence was the best comfort we could offer him.

"But if I had a straw man–"

"Yes," said Toth, "of course. Zoli can lend his name to your business. He has education, even some university education."

Again the heads turned to me.

"Sure," I said.

The man brightened. "Would you do that? I could use your help."

I nodded.

"Well," said Toth, "any more business?"

I drew in my breath and let it out.

"Yes." I stood up and faced the group. "I have an idea for making money for the orphanage and teaching the boys a skill at the same time."

"Tell us," said Toth.

"What I would like is to buy a sock machine–"

"A sock machine?" several said together.

"Please, hear me out. I know where I can get one for seven hundred forints."

"There's not that much in the church treasury, much less the orphanage fund," said one man.

I put up my hand. "If I could get some people to buy shares, for–say–ten forints each, I think the boys and I could make the machine pay for itself in less than a year."

The men considered my proposal, first silently and then in a lively debate. Toth seemed ready from the first to accept my idea, but others were more cautious.

In a while, they decided to let me try–more, I think, because I had agreed to help Kalocsai than because they wholly believed in the sock machine.

"Fine," said Toth. "That's settled. Now let's talk about the Bible conference. I think we could host it here in the new building. What do you think?"

I went about for the next few days looking for investors. The board members all bought shares, and so did Mrs. Vrabel. I put myself down for two shares against the next time I would be paid and against the hope that some shirt material would be left over to return.

I had sold twenty-eight shares, a far cry from seventy. I decided not to traipse after investors anymore but to find a way to make them come to me. I wrote an advertisement and asked the woman at the fabric shop to let me post it by the sock machine. She not only agreed to that, but she also bought a share.

Greta had taken all the fabric to her own house to work on the shirts at her own machine. We conspired then to keep the whole project secret until the start of school in the fall. Greta easily got the measurements from the shirts she laundered, and she seemed happy, if ever Greta came so near to that emotion, to be doing the work.

"You are a good man, Zoltán Galambos," she said.

Late at night, when the house was finally still and quiet, I read the Bible and prayed for wisdom in all the enterprises I found myself engaged upon. I prayed for the boys in my keeping and that I would be able to do right by them. And always I slept the sleep of the working man.

*   *   *

"All right," I said, "who thinks he can hoe this garden properly?"

"I can." Several voices came out with the same sentence.

"Well, we'll have a contest. The one who does the best on his row can have the job for the week. The rest of you will be in the kitchen."

"Let me go first."

"No, me."

I handed the hoe to the first volunteer and pointed to a row of beans, just small green leaves above the ground.

"Be careful now and don't get any good plants–just weeds."

"Zoli bacsi."

"Yes, Dani?"

"You got a lot of mail today."

He handed me a stack of envelopes. I hoped they were from people with a mind to invest in a sock machine.

One envelope brought my heart to a running pace. Milike's handwriting, like Milike herself, was beautiful and unrestrained. The letters flowed over the envelope in uneven swirls.

I went inside to read, to the window at the end of the hall.

My dear, dear Zoli,

What a shock your last letter was to me. I read it over and over to be sure I understood. And when I was sure I did, I thought about it, and nothing else, for the longest time.

I might have known, if I had listened to my wiser self and not my dreamer self, that you were from the first too good for me. I guess I knew you were noble, but I didn't think it would ever cause things to change so. I just thought it would make you a good doctor.

I am not so noble, Zoli. I want more from my life. I want to travel and have money and have time alone with the man I marry. I think that your wife would never see you much, and I know that I could not be patient with that. And I know that I would never be happy living in an orphanage or on a mission field. I look at what I've just put in writing, and I know how I must seem to you. But there it is. Perhaps telling this truth is the one noble thing I am capable of.

I hope you can forgive me. I can't come to see you. Think me a coward if you like, but what good would it do for me to come? We have goals too different to walk together. For what we were to each other, I wish you happiness and success, and I hope you can wish me the same.

Pali won't come either. He is so hurt, Zoli. Even now, I wish that you would find a way to believe him. He says he won't go to Komárom because he doesn't want forgiveness from you for something he never did.

Zoli, you are a fine man. I am not sorry to have loved you, only to have hurt you.

The letter was no surprise, but still I felt foolish, and lost, and not a little angry. But who was to blame? Who was the just object of my anger? Was Milike? She had never been anything but herself. All that she had disclosed in her letter I might have seen myself had I been looking. Was my father, for being right, for seeing his own misery in the remaking? Was God? For taking everything away from me–my home, my parents, my hope of the future, even my clothes? It seemed momentarily that I had put my life into the wrong place.

And yet, even as the bitterness rose in me, I saw Kovaly, and the new orphanage, and the faces of the boys looking up to me. And I saw the new pants I had on, and I thought of all the shoes and clothes that had come from the hand of God by others' hands, and I was ashamed. Still, that night, when I reached for my Bible, I found I could not open it.

* * *

The third night that I dismissed the boys from supper without reading to them, Mrs. Vrabel banged them to a halt with her wooden spoon and a metal pail.

"I have a little reading I want to do," she said, "from God's Word."

They all sat down again.

She laid open a large Bible and read in her strong voice from the Eighty-fourth Psalm. "This is a psalm I always liked," she said.

> *My soul longeth, yea, even fainteth for the courts of the Lord: my heart and my flesh crieth out for the living God.*

I felt the words more than I heard them.

> *For a day in thy courts is better than a thousand. I had rather be a doorkeeper in the house of God, than to dwell in the tents of wickedness.*
> *For the Lord is a sun and a shield: the Lord will give grace and glory: no good thing will he withhold from them that walk uprightly.*
> *O Lord of hosts, blessed is the man that trusteth in thee.*

I looked at my hands. I had more trust in them than in the God of hosts. I raised my head. Mrs. Vrabel was closing the book, but I knew that the matter was not closed for me.

"Boys," I said, "I have to ask you to forgive me for not doing my whole job lately. Mrs. Vrabel has reminded me of it tonight, and I hope to do better. I tell you all the time that the Lord looks after you, and then I forget it myself."

There was a long space in which no one spoke, no one moved. The boys got up gradually and went to do their chores. I glanced at Mrs. Vrabel, but she gave no sign that she had meant anything.

* * *

"Mr. Kalocsai," I said, "how much rent do you pay on this shop?"

"Fifteen forints a month."

I looked down at the books again. The light was dim in there, but I was sure the figures I had worked were right.

"Let me ask you," I said, "where you recorded that payment. I can't seem to find it listed here."

"Oh," he said, a little laugh coming out with the word, "I paid it out of my own pocket. The store didn't do very well last month."

I nodded. Or the month before, I saw, or the month before that.

"How much do you mark up the books you buy?"

"Zoltán, I'll tell you," he said, "I don't. It just doesn't seem right to charge people for these books. You know, to make a profit on the Christian friends."

I pulled my hand over my jaw. "You are in debt, Mr. Kalocsai."

"Yes, I know. But I thought that I could just sell more books. Get a bigger selection."

"What you need to do is make some money on the books you have."

He went over and stood by the window, looking out on the street.

"Now, Zoltán, I just think that's wrong. I haven't got the heart to tell somebody a book is more than it is."

I closed the ledger. I wished this man did not look so much like Kovaly.

"Then maybe it's best that you not have the store."

He turned from the window, his eyes like the eyes of a man who has seen his wheat beaten down with rain the day before harvest.

"Oh, now," he said.

"Please, sir, understand me. You could just buy books and give them away–and save the rent on the shop. Do you see how it is the same thing?"

He looked at me for the longest time. Then he dropped his gaze and nodded.

"You're right, son. I know you are. I've never worked for myself. I've no head for business. My wife has told me that."

I stood up, taking my cap from the table.

"Wait," he said. His look was pleading, pitiful almost.

"Yes?"

"Couldn't you run the store? You could make a go of it. I know you could. And I have it started."

"Mr. Kalocsai, I have more now than I–"

"Just give it a try. Just until the fall. Please."

I sighed. "You're in debt, sir. We'd need to borrow money to buy more inventory, and I'm afraid the bank won't lend you any money."

"My brother can borrow it," he said. "If I can get you 3,000 forints, will you do it?"

I thought of all the work waiting for me at the orphanage, at the church. I looked at the little room with its rough board shelves and the few books and the small window. I thought of the Bible conference Toth was planning for September. And I looked again at the man in front of me, waiting for me to speak.

"I'll try," I said. "Until Bible conference in September."

And as I shook the man's hand, I wondered where that answer had come from.

*   *   *

Gab was splitting wood. I came up the back way, and for a few moments he did not see me. He placed the wedge and tapped it with the maul. Then he drew the maul over his head and brought it down. The piece of wood sprang apart, the halves bouncing to the sides of the block.

He bent to pick them up, and then he saw me.

"Hello," he said.

"How'd everything go this morning?"

"Fine. No problems."

He balanced another piece of wood on the block.

"A professor from the Gymnásium came to see you."

"About one of you boys?"

He shook his head. "He's your friend. Professor Kovaly."

I was grieved and glad at the same time to hear that.

"I'm sorry I missed him," I said.

Gab wiped his face. "You didn't. He's waiting inside."

I felt a little knot where my heart had been only the moment before.

I went in through the kitchen and came out into the lobby. Kovaly sat in the one wooden chair the main hall had. He sat facing out the door, watching the little boys sweep the porch. His hat was on his knee, his elbows over the low back of the chair.

"Sir," I said.

He turned quickly, getting his hat and standing.

"Hello–hello, my boy."

He came toward me with his arms out. I might have reached my hand out, but he carried his hat in his right hand. I hesitated, but Kovaly seemed not to notice. He embraced me soundly and then pushed me back.

"Here you are," he said. "I thought you might come by the school, but I can see now you've been far too busy."

His face was open and his eyes bright; he looked to me then as he had that day in Szilas, full of hope and life and spirit.

"It's good to see you," I said.

"Zoltán," he said, "I'm so pleased with you. I know this can't have been easy."

There was no change in him, or if there were, it was that he was even warmer toward me.

"I want to–"

He looked at me, still smiling, waiting.

"That is, I thought you might be–"

Now he looked puzzled, but he did not change his stance.

"I apologize for acting so badly last time we talked. I–"

"What?" he said.

"I accused you of trying to ruin me. Really I don't know–I have been ashamed ever since."

Kovaly had me by the shoulder.

"No cause, son, no cause."

"I apologize if I hurt you."

"Nonsense. You didn't hurt me."

The hall seemed all at once to have sound again, the broom swishing on the porch, the boys' talking, the pans clattering in the kitchen.

"You don't hate me then?"

His eyes opened wide, and his eyebrows lifted.

"You think I would turn you out on that account? And lose all those years of investment in such good stock?"

I felt the smile start somewhere in the middle of my chest and spread through me until it came to my face.

He said, "Now tell me about the work here. What can I do to help?"

"Let's sit outside," I said.

I opened the door for him.

"I'd like to see what you think about this plan I have about buying a sock machine."

Chapter Three
Season of Growing

The needle snapped off and up into the air. It fell somewhere to the right with the tiniest clink. I leaned back in the chair and studied the machine.

"What is so hard about this?" I said.

Mrs. Vrabel came into the front hall, her heavy step announcing her.

"It's late," she said. "That's what is hard about it."

I put my hand to my brow and squeezed my eyebrows toward the bridge of my nose.

"I'm sorry," I said. "Am I keeping you awake?"

When I looked around at her, I saw that she was still dressed, still in her apron.

"Go to bed, Zoltán. The sock machine will wait until the morning, I think."

"You're right," I said.

She waited a moment more and went away. I turned back to the machine. I took out the old needle and fitted another in the groove, making the screw tight against it. I pulled the yarn through the hooks again and looked at the diagram to be sure.

The hand crank was still warm from my last effort. I gave it a spin. The needles bobbed up and down. Then the yarn drew tight and thin. I stopped the wheel before the needles bent.

"What do you want?" I whispered to the machine.

I shuffled through the papers again. I opened a knob screw more and tugged at the yarn. It came through easily. I sat up straight and gave the hand wheel a turn. A needle snapped, the eye end hanging on the yarn.

I stood up and looked down on the shiny black casing for a minute. And then I went to bed.

*   *   *

Mrs. Vrabel laid the dishcloths over the edge of the sink.

"I could use a little line over the sink," she said.

"All right." I stopped in the doorway and tried to judge the length of clothesline I would need.

She opened the closet door and put away a mop and pail and closed the door with her hip. She untied her apron as she closed the door, so swiftly that all the actions seemed to be one continuous movement.

"I'm going to meet the train," she said.

I looked from the sink to her.

"The girls are coming." She studied me as though my reaction would decide her next step.

"Oh."

She took a scarf from the peg by the door and replaced it with her apron.

"So," she said, "the two younger girls will stay with me. Ilona will stay with Mrs. Greta."

I nodded. I seemed not to have anything to say in the decision.

"The girls always come to me in the summers."

"Yes." I measured the length of the sink again with my eye. "I was thinking you had four daughters."

"Anna is married."

I remembered that Ilona was the oldest, but all experience with Mrs. Vrabel made me ask no more questions.

"I'll try to get you a line up tonight," I said.

"Good."

And she was gone, out the back door.

Gab and two other boys were waiting for me on the stairs. They looked up as I came in, their expressions hopeful.

"So," I said, "these are the apprentices?"

They did not answer, but they held their same expressions.

"Let's get going then. My tools are on the porch."

The younger boys went ahead of Gab to pick up the hammer and nails.

"And this," I said. I took the broom from beside the door.

"A broom? What for?" The look on their faces was a mixture of confusion and disgust.

"Just take it," I said.

The bookshop had not improved since I had been in it to look at the ledgers. Cobwebs still strung down from the ceiling, and the window was splotched by more rains. All the books that were left lay in piles on the two shelves.

The boys gazed around as though upon the ruins of a fire.

"This is the bookstore, huh?" said Gab.

"This will be the bookstore," I said. "There's lumber out back. Can you get it?"

Gab nodded and handed the saw to me.

"Now," I said to the other two, "let's clean this place up before we make another mess."

"Why?" said one boy.

"Because I can't think in here," I said.

Gab came in with new boards.

"What are you going to use that little room in the back for?"

"Maybe an office. But for now, well—" I looked around the door. "Mice, I suppose."

$$* \quad * \quad *$$

Dani stood with his hands in his pockets, staring at the garden rows. The tendrils of the peas snaked up the poles, the onions spiked out of the ground, and the carrots were little bunches of feathery green. I stopped when I saw him, the small farmer reviewing his work.

I laid the saw and hammer on the back step. He did not turn, or seem to hear me, so deep was he in concentration.

"Looks like a good crop coming," I said.

"Yes," he said.

Still he did not turn away from his study of the vegetables. I went to stand beside him.

"Something worrying you?"

"Not exactly."

"What then?"

He faced me finally.

"I don't know where we can put the flowers."

"What flowers?"

"The ones Miss Ilona wants to plant."

I felt my eyebrows go up. He turned to the garden again.

"Oh," I said, "those flowers."

"Maybe," he said, "we could dig another patch for her?"

He turned his eyes but not his head toward me, the smallest grin at the corner of his mouth.

"She's pretty, Zoli bacsi."

I gave him a little push with my elbow.

"What do you know about it?" I said.

"I know pretty," he said.

He moved away, as though I might come after him, looking back over his shoulder, grinning. But I did not feel like chasing him.

"Go on with you," I said. "Hey, could you put up the saw for me?"

He became again the serious Dani.

"Sure."

I took two nails and a hammer and went on into the kitchen.

I rummaged through the closet in the kitchen. I pulled out a length of twine from under a pile of rags. I leaned out and looked toward the sink and back at the twine. Too short. I went into the closet again, but I found nothing at all in the family of clothesline.

I felt there was someone in the doorway.

"This came for you," said Mrs. Greta.

She held out a large box, wrapped in brown paper and sturdy string.

"What are you looking for?" she said.

"Oh, nothing, I just forgot—"

I seized the box from her and ran my fingers under the string.

"This will do."

"What is it?"

"The string."

"What?"

I looked up and Mrs. Greta was looking down, her head tilted slightly.

"I mean I was looking for string like this."

"Oh," she said, but her head remained tilted.

"The box is the special yarn I sent for, I think."

"Oh," she said again. "When you have a minute, I want to show you something."

"All right."

I untied the string and carried it to the sink, stretching it from one side to the other. I fished the two nails out of my pocket and hammered one into a shelf on each side of the sink. Mrs. Vrabel came in as I was winding the second end onto a nail.

She looked at the line, then at me, then at the paper-wrapped box on the table.

"Will this serve?" I said.

She looked at me again.

"Good thing the package came, I guess."

Mrs. Greta came back into the kitchen, her arms full of material. She laid out two shirts on the table.

"These aren't done," she said. "The sleeves are just basted in. But I was wondering what kind of collar I should put on."

I went over to see.

"This collar is out of style," she said. "But it doesn't take as much material. And this is the new kind of collar."

She laid a collar on each shirt.

"Use the new collar," I said.

"What for?" said Mrs. Vrabel.

I said, "Because if the boys look second-rate, they behave second-rate."

"Pah," she said. "The old style is good enough. And easier to make too."

"There's not much more to making the new collar," said Mrs. Greta.

Mrs. Vrabel made the most of her height.

"An hour times thirty is thirty hours."

I turned fully toward Mrs. Greta. "The new collars," I said.

She nodded. Mrs. Vrabel stomped off toward the stove.

I took the box from the table and went into the front, pulling away the paper as I went. The box underneath said "Yarn. Six skeins."

I stopped just by the stairs. Ilona sat at the sock machine, the afternoon sun outlining her, the thick brown braids crisscrossing on the top of her head and winding on around each side. Her white collar stood up in starched perfection, but the gray sleeves of her dress were rolled up to the elbows.

She leaned forward and studied the hooks on the machine and pulled the yarn between her fingers. Her hand looked small and white against the black casing.

She raised the spool, her hand moving up like a dove to a branch.

"Hello," I said.

She half-turned away from the machine and smiled.

"Hello."

"I'm–you probably don't remember me–I'm–"

"Zoltán. I remember."

She glanced down. I thought of how Bootblack had introduced us and how she had looked down the first time we had spoken.

I rubbed my nose as though I were going to sneeze.

"That's a sock machine," I said. "Swiss. All the directions are in Swiss."

She looked back at it. "I think I have it threaded," she said.

I put the box on the steps.

"Really? Let's see."

She turned the hand wheel. The needle went up and down easily several times, and a few stitches ran out.

"Well," I said. "How about that?"

I stood up straight again, suddenly aware that I had been working in the bookstore all day.

"I–I got some yarn," I said, "to try out the machine tonight. I thought I'd try to make something."

She got up and stepped back from the chair.

I said, "No, I didn't mean right now."

I picked up the box again.

"Here it is, if you want to try," I said.

"Oh no," she said. She looked down again. "I just threaded it, kind of like a sewing machine. I wouldn't know how to make socks."

"If I get it figured out, I'll show you."

She smiled at me and went out to the kitchen.

* * *

"What is this?" I said.

"Noodles." Mrs. Vrabel looked at me as she might look at a stray cat.

"From yesterday, I take it."

"And so?"

"They've gone sour in the heat."

"They can be eaten." She tipped up her chin a little.

"No, they cannot."

She put her hands on her hips, and the wooden spoon she carried stood out from her side like a sword in a scabbard. "I say they can."

I put the bowl down with deliberate care. "Eat them then. But the boys get something else."

Her face turned red, and her mouth made a fine line.

Editke and Margarette watched from the sink, their eyes wide, saying nothing.

Mrs. Vrabel remained rooted. I would have liked to get on with my work, but I felt that leaving would be seen as retreat. I waited her out.

At last, she picked up the bowl and went back toward the stove. "You ruin those orphans, treating them like kings."

"Not kings, Mrs. Vrabel—people."

She dumped the noodles into the kettle, slammed on the lid, and carried the kettle out.

Margarette and Editke bent to their dishwashing without so much as a whisper passing between them.

"Thank you," I said.

I went out the front and sat on the steps. Dani was there, digging up the dirt along the walk.

"Zoli bacsi," he said, "this is all right, yes?"

I nodded. "Yes."

There were geraniums in a bucket beside him.

"Miss Ilona brought these on the train with her," he said.

"Did she?"

"She must really want them, to go to all that trouble."

"Does she know you're putting them here?"

He dropped his eyes.

"No. I wanted to surprise her."

His hands were dirty and his hair damp around the temples. But just at that moment I could not imagine how it was that he was here, not with those eyes, not with that heart.

After supper that evening, Dani hung around the kitchen, not following the others to the field, or even seeming to notice that they went. He sat with a book at the end of the table, reading by the yellow light of a sinking sun.

Occasionally he glanced up at me, at the papers I was going over from the day's lessons, and just as quickly went back to his book.

When at last Mrs. Vrabel hung the dishrags over the line above the sink, he got up and went around the side of the table.

"What are you going to do now, Miss Ilona?"

She smiled at him, warmer than the summer sun lingering on the garden outside.

"I thought I might mend some things," she said.

"Oh," he said.

She came near him, and for a moment I thought she might touch his hair or his cheek.

"But not right away," she said.

He looked up, as though she had told him that he was to be the next king of Hungary.

"Can you come see something?"

"I can."

He took her hand and led her through the hall door. I got up and followed, carefully distant, unable to stay in the kitchen.

The screen door swung shut, framing the two of them. Ilona put her hands up to her face, one on each side. Then she turned to Dani and took his face between her hands. She bent forward, and her mouth moved, but I did not hear what she said. Then they both walked down, to inspect the geraniums I suppose, and I did not go farther into the front to watch.

* * *

"How much longer will those girls be here?" said Feri, his white-blond hair in his eyes again. His lower lip poked out; his arms were crossed.

I laughed. "Why?"

"How long, though?"

"'Til after the Bible conference, probably."

He rolled his eyes. "That's eight more weeks!"

"What's been so bad so far?"

I tapped a nail to start it and looked over at him.

"They're in the way."

I drove the nail in with two hard blows. The sound vibrated through the little store. "How?"

"They just are."

Gab held the other end of the board steady as I tap-started another nail. He grinned at me, and I winked.

"Well, what do you want me to do? Throw them out on the porch?"

Feri suddenly giggled. "No."

I finished off the second nail and moved to Gab's end of the board.

"Look at it this way, Feri–you haven't had to do any dishes since they came, have you?"

He pondered this idea. He shifted his weight to the other leg.

"I just don't like Margarette. She bosses me around."

"Get used to it," Gab said.

I drove in the other nails. We stood away from the shelves and admired them.

"Looks good in here," I said. "Tomorrow we can put up the books, I should think."

"Can I run the store?" Feri said.

"You can help. But I thought you wanted to run the sock machine."

"Zoli bacsi?"

"Yes, Feri. I'm still here."

"Let's quit and go play soccer. It's Saturday. We spend all our Saturdays in here."

I rubbed my forehead.

"Please?" he said.

"Oh, go on then," I said.

He brightened, and then sagged momentarily.

"You come, too," he said.

I started to shake my head, but I caught a glimpse of Gab, his young man's face bearing the same look as Feri's.

I stopped myself from speaking. I took in the store with a sweeping gaze.

"Well," I said, "if we're going to waste some time, let's really waste it."

"Like what?" Feri said.

"Just get our tools, and you'll see," I said.

At the orphanage, Mrs. Vrabel just stared at me, her expression not angry, not perturbed, just blank.

"A picnic," I repeated. "Not much, just some sandwiches or something."

"Are you crazy?" she said.

"Maybe," I said. "But I think not."

"Hrummph."

"Oh, Mama," said Ilona, "let's do. We all could do with an afternoon for something besides work. I'll get the food ready. Margarette and Editke will help me."

"It's a waste of good daylight," said her mother.

"We'll work twice as hard tomorrow," said Ilona.

"Tomorrow is Sunday."

Ilona laughed outright, and I realized that I had never heard her laugh before. It made me think of Milike.

She bent over and kissed her mother on the head.

"Monday then," she said, still smiling, still with a laugh in her voice.

The excursion took us just beyond the bridge over the little river behind the orphanage property. We ate the sandwiches and the plums that Ilona had managed for us, and then I permitted soccer and swimming and races.

Late in the afternoon, Ilona came to watch the soccer game, leaving her shady seat beside her mother, and her sewing.

"This was a good idea," she said to me.

"I think it was."

"You used to play soccer up in Farna."

I waved a boy back onto the field. "Mostly I broke up fights," I said.

"Do you hear from—what did you call Miklos—Bootblack?"

I motioned for Gab to replace me on the sideline. "No," I said. "Not since last spring. Don't you?"

She blinked widely at me, as though I had said a truly odd thing. "No."

I tucked my shirt in a little better and studied the soccer field.

"I—that is—well, I thought you might."

"No."

The sun was throwing longer shadows behind the trees along the river. We stood for some time watching the boys. At least I thought she watched them.

"I guess I should call them in," I said.

Ilona said nothing. Then she nodded and wandered back toward her mother.

*   *   *

Ilona was picking beans when I came from the church Monday. She worked fast, but her movements were so smooth, the work seemed to be no effort, as though the pods leaped into the basket if she merely touched them.

I went in the row and began to pull the pods off on the other side and throw them into her basket.

"You don't have to pick beans," she said. "You have important things to be doing."

"I like beans," I said.

She smiled a little and dipped her head.

"I'm sorry if I said the wrong thing about Bootblack Saturday," I said.

"No," she said. "I just didn't understand."

I threw several pods into her basket.

"Zoli, these aren't ready," she said.

"Oh. Well, here, I'll put them back."

"Stop," she said. She laughed and hit my hand. I let go of the pods.

"Up at Farna," I said, "I got the idea Bootblack liked you."

She looked at me with those wide eyes again.

"We were friends," she said. "That's all."

My hands were fumbling over the vines. I stopped picking beans.

She said, "I didn't think you thought about it at all."

Mrs. Vrabel was suddenly in the garden.

"Ilona, Editke needs some help in the kitchen."

Ilona looked briefly at me and then handed the basket over to her mother.

When she had gone in, Mrs. Vrabel said, "I know what you're thinking, Zoltán Galambos. But you can stop thinking it. Ilona is going to be a deaconess in the church. And there's an end on it."

She thrust the basket into my hands and went back down the row, nearly running over Dani who had started into the garden.

I stood looking after her, holding the basket like a lost child.

"Zoli bacsi, what's a deaconess?"

I focused my gaze on Dani, coming to myself again.

"Son," I said, "something Miss Ilona is never going to be."

Chapter Four

Reapers

"Zoltán," said Toth, "we've not even opened the doors, and already we're nearly out of this devotional book."

He held up the two copies from the shelf.

"I've got more coming."

"How?"

"I saw how they were selling, just from people wandering in to see the shop, how we fixed it up. And I thought, well, order more now and by the time these are gone, I'll have the money to pay for the ones that come in the mail."

Toth shook his head. "If I hadn't seen before how you can make things work, I'd worry about you."

I couldn't imagine Toth worrying about anything. His nature did not seem able to hold that emotion in the same sphere with his blithe confidence. My nature, however, was not the same as his.

"And I think the conference will bring in sufficient business to pay off the first credit Kalocsai got last spring."

Toth waited for me to look up.

"You do worry Mrs. Vrabel, you know."

I smiled a half-smile. "Yes, I know."

"I don't mean with the money, exactly."

"Yes, I know."

"Should she be worried?"

I raised up from my book sorting. "What do you mean?"

"Now, Zoltán, you know me–I'm not meaning you are doing anything wrong. I mean, do you want to marry Ilona?"

I eyed him, as though I might buy him. "Who's asking?"

Toth spread his hands in front of his girth. "Just idle curiosity on my part."

I tried to frame a careful answer, but he spoke ahead of me, pushing a box of books toward the counter.

"So, will everything be ready in two days for the Bible conference?"

"Oh yes. We'll be fine. I've taught Feri to keep inventory. And I'll be here to mind the cash register."

"What about the sock adventure?" Toth grinned at me.

"You'd be surprised," I said. "Dani can make a pair almost as fast as I can." I rubbed the back of my neck. "I hate to spend money on yarn though. I've been thinking of trying to unravel the old–"

The door banged open, and Dani stood breathless before us.

"Zoli bacsi, come home! Your brother is here!"

"My brother?"

"Yes! Hurry!"

"You must have things mixed up," I said.

"No, I don't! His name is Béla Galambos and he's down at the orphanage."

I shot a glance at Toth. Then I left the shop and trotted all the way. Even from a distance I could see him on the porch, and I knew without question his stance, the awful familiarity of it, so like my father's, so like Victor's.

When he saw me, he came toward me so that we met in the road a ways from the orphanage.

His face looked strained, as though he had come to me under fire. My blood went suddenly cold to look at him.

"Zoltán–Victor had an accident."

"What?"

"The thresher. His arm."

"What happened?"

He studied the ground.

"I don't know. I was talking to him and then–I don't know what happened. It was so fast."

His eyes welled, but I could not step closer to comfort him.

Béla said, "Mama doesn't know I came here." His chest heaved.

I waited still, without the power to do anything else.

I tried to ask the question. "Is he–did he–"

Béla shook his head.

"They cut off his arm, Zoli. Two days ago. He just lies there, all white and quiet. His right arm it was."

Béla raised his eyes to mine.

"Oh, Zoli–it pulled him in! I couldn't shut it down fast enough! And it threw him against the side and back over and back again." He wiped his eyes. "Papa got him out, and there was so much blood, I–I couldn't even see his face."

He stopped, and made his lips stiff, and his face got flushed. He made a choking sound, and then a sob rushed from him. I went forward and touched his shoulder. He cried then, clutching the collar of my shirt. The smell of his hair was like the smell of our house.

"Papa wants you to come home," Béla said at last. "He sent me to get you."

I let him pull back from me.

"I'm going," I said. "There's no train out tonight, though. We'll leave in the morning."

Béla did not want to stay at the orphanage. He said he would meet me at the train station. He walked away from me, and I had a moment's urge to go after him, to ask him whether he had eaten and where he would stay, but the past was yet a wall, even now.

The boys did not talk during supper. They looked at me when they thought I wasn't looking, as though the news might have somehow changed my face. The only sounds were the clink of forks on plates and the muffled thuds of glasses being set down.

At the end of the meal, I rose and read to them as always. I read the next chapter in Romans, chapter eight, as it fell that day.

> *There is therefore now no condemnation to them which are in Christ Jesus, who walk not after the flesh, but after the Spirit.*
> *For the law of the Spirit of life in Christ Jesus hath made me free from the law of sin and death.*

I knew these words by heart. I was comforted by their sound.

> *For if ye live after the flesh, ye shall die: but if ye through the Spirit do mortify the deeds of the body, ye shall live.*
> *For as many as are led by the Spirit of God, they are the sons of God.*
> *For ye have not received the spirit of bondage again to fear; but ye have received the Spirit of adoption, whereby we cry, Abba, Father.*
> *The Spirit itself beareth witness with our spirit, that we are the children of God.*

I looked out at the faces before me and wondered whether these words struck home.

> *And we know that all things work together for good to them that love God, to them who are the called according to his purpose.*

I hesitated, reading those words again to myself. Then I read on to the end of the chapter.

> *For I am persuaded, that neither death, nor life, nor angels, nor principalities, nor powers, nor things present, nor things to come,*
> *Nor height, nor depth, nor any other creature, shall be able to separate us from the love of God, which is in Christ Jesus our Lord.*

I closed the Bible, and I let the boys go—encouraged them to go—to the field to play soccer. A few went, but many stayed and bade me with their eyes to tell them something that would put things in order again, that would take the severity from the news.

"My brother's not dead," I said. "He's just hurt. And I have to go see him."

For many this was enough, and their smiles returned, and the low talking became again the shouts and bandying of children who are free of fear.

But not so Dani, for he sat away from me at the far edge of the porch, his chin on his knees and his arms wrapped around his legs.

Ilona sat on the rocker, unravelling a worn sock and making a ball of the yarn as far as it was unbroken.

Mrs. Vrabel sat in another chair shelling peas; Editke, helping by breaking open the pods.

"Where's Margarette?" Ilona asked.

"With Mrs. Greta," said her mother.

I tried to think over everything I did in a day, to write it down for those who would have to do the work.

"Dani," I said, "come sit here and help me think, will you?"

He did not move for several seconds, and then he slowly unwrapped himself and came to me.

He plopped himself beside me on the steps and looked at the flowers.

I said, "Whom shall I ask to wake everyone up in the morning?"

He did not answer me.

"Shall we ask Mrs. Vrabel or Gab?"

"What's it like to die?"

His question silenced us. Ilona's rocker slowed, and Editke stopped humming to herself.

"I don't know, Dani, really."

"Is it like turning out a lamp?"

I gave my mind to this image, seeing it from different angles.

"To some maybe it is. But to a Christian, I think it must be more like turning up a lamp, brighter and brighter, until the light is so bright, you don't even see the lamp anymore."

Over Dani's head, I could see Ilona looking at me, with her eyes brimming and her face flushed with crying that she resisted.

"I don't want to die," said Dani. "I don't want you to die."

He still studied the geraniums. His hands gripped his knees.

Mrs. Vrabel took the pan of peas from Editke and motioned inside with her head. They both got up and went in with no more sound than a shadow. Ilona stayed in her rocker.

"Dani, you don't have to be afraid of dying, or of my dying, if you believe that Jesus died for you. If you believe that, then dying is like going home forever."

He brought his gaze to mine. "Did Kis néni go home?"

"Yes. Kis néni went home."

"In the brighter and brighter light?"

"I think it must have been like that."

"Will you go?"

"Sometime."

"Then I want to go too."

Ilona came down on the step and sat on the other side of Dani, and together we prayed, until he made sure of his first, and last, real home.

*   *   *

Béla opened the kitchen door. The house was quiet, except for the drumming of the rain on the roof. Papa sat in his chair by the window. When we came in, he stood up. His eyes were black underneath, almost as though he had been in a fight.

I nodded to him, and he to me. His glance went toward his room, and I knew that Victor was in there. The blood pounded in my head; my palms were wet, but not with rain.

I looked to Béla, but his eyes were down. I pulled up my shoulders and went to the bedroom door.

My mother sat with her back to the door, facing the bed. Victor lay on his back, his face turned away so that I could not tell whether he slept.

After a moment, my mother's shoulders stiffened slightly and her head came up just a little. Then she got up, not like herself, but like an old woman, and passed by me in the doorway, not seeing me, not wanting to, as though I were only a shadow on a wall.

I went closer to the bed. The sheets were drawn over Victor's shoulders, and his face seemed to be no darker than the sheets.

I eased down into the chair. The back creaked, and I stopped moving. A long while later Victor rolled his head to look at me. His gaze went through me like a blaze of lightning. His eyes seemed more like stones than human eyes.

"I'm so sorry, Victor."

He neither spoke nor moved. Had he had his strength, I might have had a blow from him, so hard and full of hate his look to me.

"I had to come. Don't hate me."

"Get out." His voice was deep and rough, as though he had gravel in his throat.

I dropped my look. "Please, Victor."

"Don't mock me."

I jerked my head up. "No, no–I wouldn't. You're my brother."

His lip lifted on one side.

I said, "I came because I wanted to. To see if I could–"

"You were sent for." His talking made him pant.

"Papa sent word. But I came on my own."

"What for?"

"To help, if I could."

He breathed with effort, as though it took his whole strength.

"There's no help for this."

"No, but there is for you."

His eyes narrowed.

"So you'll pray for me?"

I nodded, too surprised to answer.

There came a glinting edge to the look in his eyes. His nostrils widened, and his chest rose. His spit hit me on the back of the hand.

I stared down for a long time at the frothy mass. Then I wiped my hand slowly on the leg of my trousers.

"I still will," I said.

I went outside into the rain. I turned up my face to the pattering and stood so for some time, until I was soaked through and the water was streaming off my hair.

"Zoltán."

The voice was my father's, but low and empty of power.

I turned toward the house. He stood at the door, holding it open.

"Come inside."

The small fire in the stove made my clothes stick to me but not get dry. I took off my shirt and held it to the heat.

Papa said, "I didn't think you would come."

"I couldn't not come."

He said, "Can you stay a day?"

I nodded. "If you want me to."

He didn't answer, but I read desire in the silence.

"I could stay in the barn."

He said, "No. It will be as I say." He looked out the window. "I didn't think you'd come," he said to the rain.

The thresher sat in the field where it had the day of the accident. Béla had told me on the train that Papa would not move it or have it moved. He seemed bent on having it rust to pieces, on having it fall into the earth, without ever seeing it again.

After milking that evening, I said, "Papa, why don't you sell the thresher?"

He pulled his shoulder up as though my question had caused some pain in him. He shook his head and kept walking with the pails toward the milk house.

"I'll do it then," I said.

"No."

I wanted to know why not, but I dared not ask.

Suddenly he stopped and looked back at me.

"I let Victor borrow against the other farm to get it."

I tilted back my head and closed my eyes.

The next morning the rain stopped, but the clouds stayed, making the sun that came to us weak and fitful. My father milked the cows, and Dezső put down the straw and fed the calves. I helped, but it was as when I was little, always at a distance from my father.

Dezső went about his work without a word, his face sober and intent. When we went both at the same time toward the gate, to let the cows out, I made as though to race him for the honor. But he stopped and looked at me in confusion.

I swung open the gate and came back.

"It's all right," I said. "Everything is going to be all right."

"No, it's not," he said.

I rubbed my chin.

He said, "Mama said Victor will die, that people hurt like that die."

I sighed. "Sometimes. But Victor is young and very strong. And–well, you know the baker–how he has only one leg. He lost that leg in the war, and he lived."

Dezső shook his head. "Victor can't live without his arm."

I became aware suddenly that Papa was listening, although he was turned away from us. In all the moments I could remember having felt an emotion other than resentment toward the man, as when I had seen him from my window, bent over his plowing, or when, with the years of work and regret lining his face, he had told me, 'Be at least that rich,' I had never wanted to help him as I did now.

But I stood there in the dim light of the open barn doors and could not move. Dezső went out the other end of the barn and into the orchard. Papa picked up the pails again.

*   *   *

My mother came away from Victor rarely, usually only when she sensed I was in the doorway. Béla put out food, cheese and bread from the bakery and milk, and anyone ate when he felt like it.

The afternoon drew on, and I sat in the kitchen, watching out the window for the clouds to break apart and rearrange and block the sun again. Béla took some broth into the bedroom, and shortly brought it out again. He poured it back into the kettle.

When Papa came in again, I got up and washed the bowl that the broth had been in and put it away. Papa sat in his chair and opened the newspaper. He turned the front page half back on itself and then folded the bottom part up, as though it would not be too wrong of him to read a small section, not as wrong as reading with the whole width spread before him, as though there were no wrecked reality in this house. Long afterward I would think of this small action and wonder what other things I might have missed in my determination to be so different from him.

"I think I'll go back this evening," I said.

He nodded but did not look up from the paper.

"It says here that Parliament will restrict the employment of Jews."

I had nothing to say to that, a trouble so distant from our grief. I thought of Hevesi. I remembered the look he had given me and the weight his statement had laid upon me in the hall at Bratislava: "I do not hold it against you that you got the scholarship—I hold it against the world that you got it because I am a Jew." I shook my head to clear away the thoughts that had no place here.

"Papa."

He looked up.

I stayed on the far side of the stove, by the dry sink.

"I know you told me never to bring my Bible talk here, but I just need to tell you one thing."

His look went hard, as always before, but he did not deny me or get up.

"I found out that there is a God—who lives and cares. And I took Him at His Word, Papa. I asked Him to forgive me, and He did. And it has made life possible—now and forever."

I took a Hungarian New Testament out of my pocket. I laid it on the edge of the cupboard.

"This is for you, Papa. It is the only help I can offer to this house."

I touched the cover of the Book once more. I silently prayed that it would become the companion to him that it had been to me.

"Tell Mama and Victor and the boys I said good-bye."

*   *   *

The singing came rolling out of the church. I thought a moment about going on to the orphanage, to my room, and closing the door, not so much against everything else as in on myself. But the voices carried me closer, and then in, where the lamps glowed warm.

It was the last song of the evening. Ilona played the mandolin. Her fingers moved over the strings as graceful as moths, and her foot kept time with the smallest movement. When she saw me, she smiled brighter, at least it seemed so to me, and then looked down.

I waited at the door, hoping to walk with her, but Dani and Gab found me.

"Miss Ilona says we should dry some of the beans," said Dani, "and the peas, there are so many."

"I told you that you were a farmer at heart!"

Gab broke in. "Feri and I sold books so fast that we couldn't even count the money until the end of the day."

"And," Dani said, "we sold fourteen pairs of socks. We have to make some more. And some for ourselves yet too."

I said to Gab, "Did you put out more books?"

"Not yet. There wasn't time. I didn't even eat yet."

"Well," I said, suddenly hungry, "I haven't either. Let's see what's left."

Ilona was in the kitchen, making sandwiches.

"How did you know?" I said.

She smiled. "Safe bet."

She poured milk for the boys and made tea for me.

"And there's a little cake left," she said.

"Cake?" I could not imagine what would make Mrs. Vrabel part with that much sugar.

"I made it," said Ilona. "For a treat. The boys have worked so hard."

Dani beamed up at her, and I imagine that had I had a mirror, I might have seen that I did not look much different.

Her expression deepened, and she asked me without speaking how it was with me, with Victor. I nodded to her briefly.

Gab pulled a paper out of his back pocket.

"Look at this," he said. "One of the preachers had this Spanish newspaper. Look at these planes the Germans have."

He spread the paper out on the table. The drawing was indeed impressive.

"Think what it must be like to fly in one of those," he said.

* * *

The last day of the conference was a bright September day, the kind with the cloudless blue sky and the air rich still with summer and the smell of hay and late flowers.

The bookstore had kept me busy during the day when the preaching was not going on, and the sock machine had occupied Dani and me in the evenings and me into the small hours. But this last day I took for myself.

Ilona turned from her work at the sink.

"Do what?"

"Go with me for a boat ride. I know someone who will lend me a boat, and we could go down that stream where we had the picnic."

She continued to look at me without speaking again for some time. It gave me the feeling that the decision for her included more than an afternoon on the water.

"Just a minute," she said, and went out.

She came back, her cheeks slightly pink.

"We must take Editke and Margarette."

"Fine," I said.

She smiled. "I'll find the girls."

It was quiet on the stream, like the quiet I remembered in the libraries and halls of a far other stream, one that flowed on without change despite my not being in it any more.

The water lapped against the boat with little slaps. I rowed slowly, being in no great hurry. Margarette trailed her fingers on the water and was uncharacteristically quiet. Ilona sat at the other end of the boat, facing me.

Editke said, "Can I row a while, Zoli?"

"Zoli bacsi or Mr. Galambos," said Margarette.

"Can I?" she said again to me.

"No," said Ilona. "Not today."

After a while, I said, "What is a deaconess, exactly?"

Ilona blushed and dropped her gaze to the ripples Margarette made in the surface of the water.

"A servant of the Lord," she said.

I leaned into the oaring, more than I had to for the speed I wanted. I thought that I would not change things so much for Ilona. There were many kinds of service to the Lord.

Much further downstream, I put the boat ashore. "Let's walk a while."

Editke came and took my hand. "I'll walk with you."

I smiled in spite of the disruption of my plans.

Wildflowers grew in abundance here, and Margarette went ahead of us, scooping them toward herself by the armful and putting her face into the crowd of them.

I picked two large bouquets of white and yellow flowers and gave one each to Editke and Margarette. They danced around with them and called to Ilona, "Look, Lona, see what we have."

Ilona had gone to walk along the stream, looking into it as if for something lost. She raised her head and laughed at her sisters. She was more graceful than the water swirling by her.

The shadows stretched longer, a warning to me that time was short.

"Let's be going back," I said.

When Ilona got into the boat, I held out one bright blue flower to her.

"What's this?" she said.

"A forget-me-not."

"Oh," she said.

We were nearly back to the orphanage, walking through the field behind the garden, when Editke came around in front of me.

"I thought you liked Ilona," she said.

"I do." I cast a glance at Ilona, who was looking a threat at Editke.

"Then why," said the child, "did you give such big bouquets to me and Margarette and only one blue flower to Lona?"

I looked directly down at her.

"I gave you two the big bouquets because I like you. But–"

I turned to Ilona.

"I gave the one blue flower with love."

For once Ilona's eyes did not go down from mine.

"Ilona, will you be my wife?"

There was a moment where everything in the universe seemed to hold a collective breath.

Editke's eyes got round. She broke for the house.

"Mama! Mama! Guess what happened!"

Ilona stood in the field, the blue sky dropping behind her, the blue flower in her hands, her blue eyes shining.

She said, "The Lord willing and if Mama has no objections."

"Thank you," I said.

*   *   *

Late that night, after the last service, after the boys were long asleep, Ilona came out to the porch. She stood by the rail, and made me know, by no visible sign, but by some other communion, that I was to stay seated.

"Mama agrees," she said.

"I'm glad."

"But I haven't any money," she said, "to buy linen. And I can't marry without a dowry."

"I don't care about that," I said.

"I do," she said. "It is the custom."

Her voice, though still soft, still like evening itself, had a strength now. It made me think of being on the water and feeling the pull of the current on the oar.

"All right."

"I'll need three years to get enough money together," she said.

I tried to think.

"Is that too long?" she said.

"What will you do?"

"Find some work. I can sew by hand well enough."

I stood up. She did not move, but I felt that she gave up her resolve to direct the conversation.

"I was thinking," I said. "Feri and Gab will be back in school, and the bookstore will be without a clerk."

She laughed a little laugh.

"How much does it pay?"

"How much is a dowry?"

Chapter Five
Restoration

February, 1938

I pushed open the door of the little room in the back of the bookstore. The warmth of a one-lid stove filtered out to us. On the window, the blue curtains from the machine of Mrs. Greta hung to the floor. A quilt in blues and whites from many women's hands lay over the bed.

"Oh," said my wife, "it's so pretty."

I smiled at her, in wonder, at her wonder–at her pleasure in so meager a house, this one room with one window, and a bookstore weighting it down.

"And you've painted it so nice, Zoli."

She stepped in and went from chair to window to dresser, touching everything lightly. She turned her bright look to me, and I knew that every beautiful thing that I had ever seen before this had been nothing, nothing at all.

"It's just for a while," I said.

"It's a fine and happy place," she said.

"Now it is," I said.

* * *

Toth stood up from the desk in the church office.

"Zoltán, what are you doing here? A man married on Saturday doesn't have to be at work on Monday."

"A man with thirty children does," I said, and he laughed. "What are you doing here?"

"Well, I was going to do your work, but since you're here, I have some visits I could make. Where's Mrs. Galambos?"

"Minding the store. We don't have enough house for her to keep. At least not all day."

He laughed again. "All right. I'm off then. Oh, I have been meaning to ask–some of the sock machine investors want to know if you would take back the dividends you sent them?"

"They can't use a pair of socks–better made than any in the stores?"

"Sure, sure, they could. But they are satisfied to have their investment returned. They want to donate the socks to your sale inventory."

I nodded. "That's very kind."

He stuck out his hand and I took it, and then he left, at his usual full tilt, always remarkable to me in a man of his size.

"You left your–"

I heard the door close soundly.

"Newspaper."

I sat down and unfolded it. On the front page, in a side column, as though not of too great import, was a small title: Austria Accepts Nazi Minister of Interior.

The first sentences caused my heart to pound. "Chancellor Schuschnigg, after a meeting with Adolph Hitler, the leader of

Germany, has announced that Austria will accept a Nazi as Minister of Interior. The Chancellor also said that Austria will begin granting amnesty to imprisoned Austrian Nazis.''

"What are they thinking?" I said to the walls.

The next sentence might have made me laugh, had the absurdity not been so near catastrophe. "In a revival of his former policy of independence, Schuschnigg implied that he would call for a popular vote in Austria to ratify this compromise.''

I wondered what Professor Fenyo was asking his history classes this day in Bratislava. I was sure he was stalking the aisles of his room, throwing this news under the students' noses, and demanding that they learn to read it, and read into it.

I put the paper aside and pulled out the ledgers. But I found I could not put away the apprehension as easily as the newspaper.

* * *

March came in mild. From the roads and then the banks and even the high places, snow disappeared with quiet swiftness, like deer retreating to the woods at dawn, leaving only pressed grasses and still fields behind.

The earth leveled itself this spring, filling every low place with water, drawing the sky into the mirrors formed there, erasing the distance between the land and the blue-whiteness over it.

Ilona came nearly to me, stopping just behind me, as though she would only look over my shoulder at this private desolation.

"What is it, Zoli?" she said.

I could not look away from the wet earth for some time.

"It's nothing," I said at last. "I just have never liked the spring, that's all.''

I thought she might ask me why, or tell me there was no reason not to—but she only took my hand and looked out with me upon the separate pools here and there among the old grass and the new weeds.

"Your letter home came back today," she said.

I nodded. "The mail is very regular."

"I put it with the others."

"I thought Béla might answer," I said.

"Perhaps he never sees your letters."

"Perhaps."

"I'm sure Victor is all right. Surely they would tell you if not."

"He's alive. He's not all right." The melancholy of the season and the returned letter made my voice hard.

I felt her head lower a little, like a flower under too much sun.

"I'm sorry," I said. "I'm not angry."

She put her arm through mine and rested her head on my shoulder. I trembled, again, at this response, at the proof of her connection to me. I had not known before what it was to have a heart beat to mine.

"I thought," she said, "that if you want, I would invite the Kovalys for supper sometime."

Her blue eyes looked up at me, and I knew that she had sought the one thing she might offer to cheer me and recompense me a little for the letter.

* * *

"Gab," I said, "be serious."

"I am. I'm seventeen until next week, and then they'll take me."

"But why the army?"

He hefted the axe and brought it down on the wood for answer.

I said, "I thought you were happy here."

He looked at me in a way that made me think of Pali, and for a fleeting time, I felt younger than the boy in my charge.

"The boy of me is," he said. "But I need to be on my way."

He chopped away another block from the log, the chips flying around him.

I swung my axe against the log and made a deep gash in the even bark. I swung again, and a slice like a smile opened up, white in the gray trunk.

"Hungary's army, I hope," I said.

"In Budapest," he said.

"So you are serious."

"I leave the end of the month."

We worked the log until it was five blocks ready for splitting. I struck my axe into another log and left its handle sticking up.

"Keep your boots polished," I said.

* * *

Kovaly put his cup down and moved aside his plate.

"That was wonderful, Ilona. Zoltán did all right for himself."

"Henrik," said his wife.

He reached out and patted her hand, but he spoke to me. "I seem to have forgotten all the instructions I received on our walk here."

Ilona laughed a little and got up to clear the table.

We ate rather late, having waited for the boys to have their supper and go out. I could hear them yelling to each other.

"I think you unnerve the Gymnásium boys when you come here to dinner," I said.

Kovaly ran a finger over his mustache, and his eyes twinkled.

"Probably only those behind in their work."

"Some are behind?" I leaned forward in my chair.

Kovaly waved his hand.

"No, no, Zoltán. Easy, now. The boys from the orphanage are among my best students."

I sat back, as though from much labor, and let my head rest on the tall chair.

Ilona smiled over at me from the sink. The light fell on her hair, and the kitchen was quiet. I looked back at Kovaly, and I knew, in one of those uncommon grantings of insight, that this one moment I would carry with me until I died. I set it to memory: the sounds of the children outside and the clink of the dishes in the sink, the faces of Kovaly and his wife and Ilona, the sense that here was nearly perfect happiness, here was a crowning for a man's life, whether he lived one day more or a hundred years.

Kovaly and I went out to sit on the porch. I moved the newspaper I had been scanning earlier and gave my old teacher the rocker.

The paper flopped open. I held it out to him, the headline–Germany Annexes Austria Without Contest.

"What do you think this means?"

The white head shook slowly.

"I can't say," he said. "Perhaps the Rhineland and Austria are all he wants."

I folded the paper. The air was cool, but not for March.

"Gab is leaving the end of the month."

He nodded. His eyes did not leave me. "It's hard to let them go."

I sat down on the step. Kovaly did not rock the chair or say anymore. The sun was nearly down, balancing on the horizon like a bubble on the surface of the water. I willed it not to go under, but it went. The lights from the doorway brightened behind us. Henrik Kovaly began to move the rocker in a slow and even rhythm.

*   *   *

"Zoli bacsi, will you let me have charge of the garden this year?"

Dani's head now came nearly to my shoulder.

"You are completely qualified?"

He nodded vigorously. Then he blushed a bit and looked at his toes.

"I remember what you taught me last year."

"Well, after I look over what's up already, we'll discuss it."

He stood there a minute more and then grinned and dashed away.

I said to Ilona, "Why do I feel I've already lost my garden?"

She patted my face. "You never had a chance."

Mrs. Vrabel turned from the stove, her cheeks red from the heat of the cooking and the early summer weather.

"He always was that way," she said. "It's his gift."

I stared at the woman. Sometimes she was possessed of a most inspiring wisdom and graciousness.

"What's mine?" I said.

She said, "Marrying well."

I grabbed Ilona and pulled her to me. "That's true," I said.

Editke and Margarette giggled into their cups of milk.

"I have to get to the store," Ilona said. But she did not try to get away.

A solid knocking sounded at the front door.

"Who's so early?" Mrs. Vrabel said.

I drew back the door on a uniformed man.

"Yes?"

"Zoltán Galambos?"

"Yes."

He handed me a letter. "I'll wait for a reply."

I let the door shut behind me and opened the letter. I took in the words quickly. Then I looked up, directly at the fellow.

"I'll answer in person. Where is your commanding officer?"

A voice, one I knew well, said, "Here."

And suddenly, there was Bootblack–Lieutenant Nandor now–on the stones of the walk.

"That will be all," he said to the soldier beside me, and the man went down the steps and away.

I too went down the steps and took the hand of my oldest friend, my heart's brother.

After a moment, I found my voice.

"I thought you were a schoolteacher."

"That was my plan," he said. "God had another."

I clapped his shoulder and waved a hand at the building behind me.

"Yes," I said. "I have learned that lesson too."

Bootblack grinned at me. "I hear you're married."

"You hear right. Come in, come in. How did you get through the Czech barriers in that uniform?"

"A man can visit his friends still."

It seemed impossible to me that my old schoolmate, the boy from the train with holes in his socks, was sitting across from me now, in a uniform and boots, an officer. I imagined it seemed as strange to him to find himself across from me, and my wife, in another orphanage.

He said, "Then this new recruit arrives. I find out he's from Komárom. I say, 'I used to go to school there. I had this professor named Kovaly.' Well, don't his eyes get wide! 'I had that teacher,' he says."

Ilona poured the tea and sat down again.

"Then I find out that you're here, and Ilona–how about that? I started asking questions, of course." He shook his head and laughed. "Gab's a good boy, Zoli, but he's not much for social details, is he?"

He asked about our wedding, and the work in the orphanage, and the boys. When he asked about my family in Szilas, I realized suddenly that my last letter had not been returned.

We passed an hour with the details and still so much was left to say, so much life had not been told, could not, perhaps, be told.

Bootblack pulled his hat toward him on the table.

"It's not just a lark that I'm here," he said. "I already had orders to come to Komárom when I ran into Gab."

"What's happening?"

"Well, maybe nothing, maybe something."

He leaned back, taking his hat with him. He ran his fingers along the shiny bill.

"Horthy has been invited to meet with Hitler. In Hamburg in August."

"I read that."

"Nothing might come of that. But if Horthy can get back some of what we lost at the Treaty of Trianon, we want to be ready."

"You think he'll join Hitler?"

"No, I don't. But Horthy is practical, if nothing else."

I turned to Ilona. "We used to have this argument at the Gymnásium, about Hungary getting back together."

"Not an argument," said Bootblack, "a discussion."

"So what are you doing here?" I said.

"Visiting my friends."

I tipped my head and looked at him.

He said, "Some things a lieutenant keeps to himself. But I can tell you this. I got this rank very quickly because I have a Gymnásium education. It makes the regular soldiers unhappy to be passed by the likes of me, but there it is."

He leaned forward, putting his elbows on the table.

"If Komárom comes back to Hungary, Horthy will want reservists here. Zoli, you could easily pass induction, be an officer."

"Why should I do that? I have more jobs now than you know of."

"It might come to not being a choice someday. It's better to be ready, yes?"

I glanced at Ilona. Her eyes were fixed on Bootblack.

I said, "You are talking war already?"

"No. Change. I'm talking change. Nothing is going to stay the same, I think. But if you get established, if you were top officer, you could stay in Komárom with Ilona and the boys."

I took Ilona's hand but looked at him. "Nothing has happened since Austria. Perhaps nothing will. There is plenty of time to think of such things."

"Sure," said Bootblack, looking at Ilona and back at me. "Of course." He shifted as though he might stand. "Does Kovaly live where he always did?"

"He does."

"Then I want to stop there too. And I haven't much time of my own."

"Will you come back to dinner?" Ilona said.

"Another time," he said. "I'm sorry. But Hungarian officers don't have much liberty in Czechoslovakia."

He stood up then and put out his hand to me.

"Until another time."

I took his hand. "Yes. And thank you. Look after Gab, will you?"

"Sure I will."

It seemed so long since we had been boys.

* * *

I closed the door of the closet off the kitchen.

"What's in there?" Feri said.

"What is it, Zoli bacsi?"

"When can we see?"

I raised my hands to quiet the tumult of boys around me.

"After supper," I said, "you'll get your surprise. Now be off with you–all of you."

They went, but not immediately and not quickly, looking back a couple of times, in case I should have started to open the door again.

When they were gone, Mrs. Vrabel said, "Why not just tell them you bought a radio?"

"No, let them enjoy the suspense a while."

Ilona said, "You think they enjoy the suspense?"

"Of course. I don't like to know a thing right away, do you?"

She looked at me with puzzlement, but she did not answer.

When the chores were finished, and supper cleared away, I read a Psalm. Then, when I thought the tension had built sufficiently, I pulled the cover from the radio and switched it on.

The boys exclaimed together in a sound that made me think of the wind in the pines. A scratchy voice came into the kitchen and held us all silent.

"A grand parade," it was saying. "Hundreds of troops and tanks, motorcars and motorized artillery streamed past the reviewing platform. Admiral Horthy, wearing the many decorations of his long service, stood beside the German leader, watching the parade."

The boys' faces told me this had been a satisfactory surprise.

The voice went on. "Afterward the Admiral and his wife were given a gala reception on board the *Grille,* the favorite yacht of Adolf Hitler."

The news ended shortly after and music came on, a folk song I had not heard for many years.

"This music makes me think of something that happened to me when I was in school," I said.

I switched off the radio, but the promise of a story diminished most cries of disappointment.

"Do you remember that officer that visited here last month? Well, he and I were on a train one winter, and the snow was so bad, and the weather was so cold that the wheels froze fast to the tracks. . . ."

* * *

I woke to shouting and bells ringing. I sat upright, my heart pounding. Ilona had hold of my arm.

"What is it?" she said.

"Stay here."

I went out through the store and unbolted the door. Men and boys were running past me. Someone fired a pistol, and someone began the national anthem of Hungary in a deep and rugged voice.

"Nem, nem, soha!" they cried. *"Nem, nem, soha!"*

"What is this?" I yelled out.

A man paused briefly. "Czechoslovakia is broken! Without a shot!"

I sucked in a breath. The September morning was crisp, and when I let the breath out, I could see it.

Ilona still sat in the bed, waiting. "What's happened?"

I got my trousers on as I answered. "Czechoslovakia has apparently been annexed by Germany."

"What does that mean to us?"

"I don't know yet. I'm going to the orphanage to hear the radio."

The covers flew back, and her bare feet hit the floor. "Not without me!"

Mrs. Vrabel and several of the older boys were already circled around the radio. They looked up as we came in, but no one spoke. A man's voice crackled through the kitchen.

"Italian radio has announced that Mussolini and Hitler have arbitrated a new agreement on the division of Czechoslovakia."

Mrs. Vrabel looked at me with dark eyes. The boys also looked to me, but I had nothing to say.

"The leaders of France, Germany, Italy, and Great Britain are in Munich to sign the agreement."

"What will happen?" Dani said.

"What God wills," I said.

*   *   *

Bootblack returned, with Hungarian troops this time, to dismantle the Czech barriers on the bridge of Komárom. Dozens of soldiers tipped up the logs that crisscrossed each other like so many tumbled toothpicks.

It poured rain the first two days of the work, but the troops seemed not to notice. The logs disappeared and were chopped to kindling and burned in every stove in Komárom. They gave off a more than satisfactory warmth.

The day the bridge was finally cleared, Bootblack came to supper at the orphanage. The boys hung off the railings of the stairs and out from behind doors to stare at him and his big wool coat with the brass buttons and his wide leather belts and shoulder straps. He grinned at them as he came in, stomping his boots.

I took his coat.

"They insisted that we eat when they did," I said. "They want to hear you talk."

He laughed his laugh. I had forgotten the joyousness of it.

Over the whisperings going on around us at supper, he told me that much of the Czechoslovakian land that had been Hungary would be Hungarian again. This news he gave me with the air of a man who has held a position that has proved wrong and now expects to hear about it.

"Where do I sign up to be a reservist?" I said.

He regarded me with friendly suspicion a moment. Then he saw that I was in earnest.

"I'll get you the papers," he said. "When Horthy's man comes here, be where you can be seen. You have the credentials. Just let them see you have the wherewithal as well."

I nodded. Ilona was quiet, asking only if more food or tea was wanted. Bootblack consented to telling stories about Zoli bacsi in his younger days, and for once, the radio was forgotten.

Feri said, "Why does Zoli bacsi call you Bootblack?"

Bootblack laughed and leaned in toward the boys like a conspirator.

"He has always resented the fact that I can darn a sock faster than he can."

He winked at me.

"Somebody bring me a tin of black shoe polish and I'll show you."

*   *   *

"Ilona, a reservist is not like a professsional soldier. I would most likely do battle with papers and figures–not Germans. But I don't want to argue. This is what I've said I will do."

She smoothed the dough out with her fingers and nodded.

I said, "I'll be at the church until the boys come home from school."

She did not answer me or look at me.

"Ilona?"

Still she did not respond, and then a tear fell to the dough, a swift glistening between her cheek and the table.

I went around to her and made her look at me.

"Ilona? What is it? You don't have to worry so. Everything will be fine. I'm grateful to Bootblack for looking ahead for us this way."

She worked the dough again.

"Yes, Zoli."

I put her chin up again with my finger. She still looked down, her lashes shiny with tears. I waited, and at last she raised her eyes and smiled a small, brave smile.

Later in the morning, Ilona came to the church, to the office. I got up from my ledgers and books and went to her. She was not sad or weary or anything that I recognized. She held out a small package.

"This just came," she said. "From Szilas."

I unwrapped it, the string around it tangling and tearing the paper. In a small box was a gold wedding band and a letter folded several times. "Zoltán" was written on the outside of the letter, in my mother's hand.

I stood for some time, just holding the box, until Ilona touched my hand.

"You read it," I said. "Read it to me."

She hesitated and then took up the letter.

"Zoltán," she said, and glanced up at me. I nodded, and she went back to the letter. "Your father died the day before yesterday."

I took a breath, and she stopped. I nodded again.

"Béla found him in the barn, but he died in his bed that evening. I am writing because I promised him I would. He said, 'Write Zoltán. Tell him I went out his way.' "

I tightened my jaw, and yet the sob jerked from me. Ilona could not read on for several seconds.

"He gave Béla the book or I would have returned it. The ring is a gift to your wife. It was my father's. Theresa Galambos."

Ilona opened her arms, and her face was wet when she took me to her shoulder.

* * *

There was no school the day Horthy came. We were all there, every man, woman, and child of Komárom, spread out through the fields on either side of the bridge. The sun was bright, but the air was cold. Dani stood beside me, and as I waited and watched with the others, it occurred to me that at all the momentous turns,

Dani had been there–at Kis néni's funeral, at my wedding, and now. I looked down at him and wondered what God had planned for this child.

A rider came over the hill, his coat flying.

"They're coming! They're coming!"

And shortly they did come, line upon line of Hungarian soldiers, marching behind the man on horseback. It was the early memory: the solemn man, his black boots a *V* in the stirrups, his white horse bobbing and snorting.

The cheering began as they made the far end of the bridge, and rose like thunder as they crossed it. I know I yelled for joy; I could feel my throat ache with the effort. But I could not hear my voice, or Dani's, or Ilona's, so lost were all in the roar of a people returned to their homeland.

We fell in behind the soldiers and cheered Horthy, the noble man who got us back our territory without losing our good name. We were Hungarians again, in the great line down from Árpád, alone and independent, in a world fast crumbling to darker forces. We had not forgotten what it meant to be Magyar.

"It was so strange," I said to Ilona that evening. "Everything was so different from when I was a child, and yet so much the same."

I pulled off my shoes.

"I should polish these," I said. "I only wish I could write Papa and tell him what I saw, and what I remember."

She came near and put her hand on my head.

"Zoli, would you care awfully if we traded your mother's ring?"

"What? What for? Why would you–"

She put her fingers to my mouth and smiled down on me.

"We're going to need some things. Like a cradle."

Chapter Six
Interim

March, 1939

Mrs. Kovaly took the baby from Ilona and cuddled him into the crook of her arm. Kovaly leaned over her and touched the little head gently.

"What's his name, Zoltán?"

Ilona and I smiled at each other.

"Zoltán Henrik," I said. "We'll call him Henrik."

Henrik Kovaly stood up, his mouth in a circle, as though he would say "oh" but had forgotten how.

Mrs. Kovaly beamed, first at us, then at the baby, then at her husband.

"Thank you," she said. "That is so wonderful of you."

Kovaly came to life. "Yes, my dears, thank you for the honor. I shall try to live up to it," he said.

"That's not how it works," I said.

Zoltán Henrik Galambos wrinkled up his face and squirmed in his blankets.

"Here comes the crying," I said.

Mrs. Kovaly stood up. "Maybe he's getting tired," she said. "Shall I put him down?"

"I'll take him," Ilona said.

"I'll take him," said Mrs. Vrabel.

Henrik gave a couple of little cries, to crank up, and then wailed.

"Shhh," said Mrs. Vrabel, "Grandmama has you."

She put him to her shoulder and patted him, carrying him toward the kitchen. Ilona watched, as mother cats watch children carrying the kittens around.

"Call me, if you need me," Ilona said.

"What do the boys think of him?" Mrs. Kovaly asked.

"I have a time already," I said. "The child never gets a chance to cry. Someone is always right there to pick him up–Grandmother, Dani, Mommy. And soon two aunts will be here to spoil him the rest of the way."

"Well," said Mrs. Kovaly, "a week won't spoil him."

Ilona said, "Thank you." And she looked at me as if to say I told you.

The crying faded in the kitchen.

Mrs. Kovaly and Ilona put their heads together, discussing the art of rearing sons, I suppose, or whatever seasoned mothers and new mothers seem always to be putting their heads together to discuss.

I tried to tell Kovaly that I had been looking for another place to live, since with the addition of a baby, the one room had suddenly become remarkably crowded.

"It seems impossible," I said, "that someone so tiny takes up so much space."

Kovaly acknowledged the joke with a smile. But he looked sober, and had looked so, as though he were not able to put his mind fully away from something.

Kovaly said, "Zoltán, I wonder whether I could have a word with you."

I motioned him toward the sock machine at the other side of the front hall. He seemed to weigh his words a long time.

"Son, I hope you won't be upset with me, but I took the liberty of looking into a situation you probably consider closed, and perhaps you want it to remain so, but nonetheless—"

"What situation?"

He put his hand up. "Last November, I received a letter from Pali's father."

I felt the color coming into my face. I shifted away from the window I had leaned against.

Kovaly said, "We are acquainted from long ago—he lived here, you may remember, until he sold the house and stayed in Budapest."

I shrugged at this news.

"He knew I had some connections at the University in Bratislava, and he asked me to find out what I could about—about the trouble there—you understand."

I did, but I said nothing.

"Since nothing was ever said to Pali about the matter, his father had no reason, or right, to inquire on your behalf."

"He needn't have."

"Well, he thought it odd that Pali was never involved officially. And so did I. I wrote an old schoolmate who teaches there and asked him to find out what he could. Two days ago, I got word from him."

"What difference does this make now?"

"I'm not talking about Bratislava, Zoltán. I'm talking about you. This is not a formal thing at all. My friend just asked a few questions."

I half-turned away from him and studied the floor.

"The report about you was filed by a clerk in the head office."

"So?"

"Hevesi."

I jerked my head up. Kovaly kept staring straight at me.

"Think of that," he said.

"Hevesi." I heard myself say the name, but I still could not take in fully what all was revealed by it. And yet, even as I stood there, I could feel the truth of it, see with the clarity of distance and time what pride and anger had kept obscure.

"He hated me that much."

Kovaly waited for some time without speaking. Then he looked at the yarn running through the rings on the machine beside him.

"You could open this again, try to clear your name."

I shook my head. "What for?"

Kovaly did not answer.

I said, "Where is Pali now?"

"He's at the University."

"And Hevesi?"

He nodded. "Still there as well."

Kovaly studied me as he had the machine. He looked back at the yarn and put his hand under a strand.

"When you get old and look back," he said, "you can see how everything is connected, even over long spaces."

"So you think I should write Pali again."

He looked up at me. "I just know from experience that it pays to keep the yarns straightened out."

* * *

The man did not look like a reservist officer. He was short, and his face made me think of a rabbit's, his nose and mouth close together and white hair pulled back from his wide temples.

He looked up and down the line of us who had distinguished ourselves in the examinations, our gold sleeve bands shining. He walked down the line then to see us face to face.

When he came to me, I looked him directly in the eye. He stopped and returned the look and then went on. He leaned away and said something to the young man with him, and the sergeant wrote on his clipboard. At the end of the line, he made a military turn and stepped back to his desk.

The sergeant said, "Wignar, Barany, Galambos. Step forward."

We did, and waited again, while the officer leafed through papers and glanced at us occasionally. At last, he took the clipboard from the sergeant and wrote on it quickly. He thrust it back to the young man and took up his hat.

"Thank you, gentlemen," he said, and left.

The sergeant studied the board in his hand. "Galambos and Wignar remain. The rest are dismissed," he said.

The others regarded us silently. Some, I knew, had been working for the rank years and years, and as they went out, I felt they would have liked to take Wignar and me with them, for a sort of congratulatory row in the back alley.

"Wignar," the sergeant was saying, "you are assigned to Kassa. You will report there immediately."

The man nodded. As the sergeant spoke, he tipped the board, and I scanned it for my name. Beside it were the words *good jaw*. I put my hand to my face in a fleeting moment of incredulity.

"Galambos, you are to remain here. Second in command to Captain Lotz."

The joy that had been rising in me suddenly washed back. I saw Ilona's face the day I had said I would join, and I remembered how I had been so sure that I would win the safe position.

"That is all, sergeants," the young man said.

I stepped onto the porch at the orphanage and was instantly swarmed by the boys and Editke and Margarette.

"What happened, Zoli bacsi?"

"What did they say to you?"

"Are you staying here, Zoli bacsi?"

I pointed to my shoulder.

"Sergeant Zoli to you."

They cheered so that I might have begun to think myself a second Horthy. Ilona appeared in the doorway with Henrik on her arm. He sat there, weaving slightly, and smiling.

Over the clamor around me, I said to her, "Komárom."

The change in her expression was so subtle I could not tell just what formed it, as when a rose opens slightly in an hour and looks a little changed and yet the same.

I took Henrik and gave Ilona a hug. I thought then that the war, if there were a war, would not come to Komárom. And I decided not to tell her that I was only second in command, for the worry would outweigh the cause, I was sure.

* * *

The last of the harvested vegetables lay on the table. Mrs. Vrabel stood by the sink, her hand to her mouth. Ilona sat at the table with a bowl half full of late berries, the hull of one still in her fingers.

The radio voice said, "About four o'clock this morning, German airplanes launched an attack against Poland. Armored divisions have since crossed the Polish borders."

The sun was going down in a wash of red, making everything outside seem as though it were standing in the glare of an awful fire.

"Regent Horthy and Premier Teleki have refused the German demand that Hungary allow an attack on Poland through the northern border."

The voice went on, and I tried to listen, but I could not. Even after the music had returned, winding about the kitchen with its pathetic gaiety, I stood in the doorway, trying to remember what

I had been told about the Great War, about the war that divided Hungary, about the war that was, we had always thought, the last battle.

Henrik clapped his hands and rolled around on his blanket. He cooed at us, but we could not find it in ourselves to answer.

Two days later Great Britain and France declared war on Germany. We knew almost as soon as it was announced, because we had left the radio on almost constantly. The boys no longer begged to be allowed to have it on during supper.

"I hate that radio," Feri said.

"Let's turn it off while we eat," said Dani. "Can't we?"

I switched the radio off. The silence settled around us, like leaves to the ground, and the relief was nearly tangible.

Dani took over the sock machine almost completely, and Ilona ran the bookstore. I still did the church books and oversaw schoolwork, but most of the time I was an officer. We all worked and lived as we had, but not without a sense of temporariness, as though always striving to use the last light before sunset.

*   *   *

"What do you think?" I said.

Ilona came out of the bedroom and went into the kitchen.

"It's so spacious," she said. "Are you sure we can afford this?"

"Zoli bacsi couldn't, but Sergeant Galambos can."

"It's wonderful–a room for Henrik, and my own kitchen!"

She had her hands clasped under her chin as she spoke, as though in a constant thankfulness.

"Look," I said.

I snapped a switch and the lightbulb in the ceiling blazed.

Ilona ran to me and kissed me soundly. I had to laugh.

"This is a 'yes,' I take it?"

"Yes, yes, yes!"

It was not much to moving us in—one bed, one dresser, two chairs, and a crib. And the move was not far, just a street from the store one way and two streets from the orphanage the other way.

Toth came and brought us a table, and his wife gave Ilona a cloth for it. Mrs. Greta, once again, produced curtains and a quilt for Henrik's crib.

In the month it took us to find the place, move in, and settle down, Germany overran Poland, divided it with Russia as calmly as the rest of us sliced bread, and sat in smug possession that October of much more of the world than anyone had believed possible.

We sat down, Ilona and I, to have our first meal alone since we had been married, at our own table, in our own house. I could not have imagined the pleasure I felt at that moment. To have something that is entirely your own, and entirely your own responsibility, is like breathing clear air.

Henrik cried from his crib, a long and hearty wail. Ilona stood up.

"Sit down, Ilona."

She stared at me and remained standing.

"Henrik—"

"Henrik's blackmailing days are over," I said.

"What are you saying?"

"He ran the orphanage, and he ran us when we had only the one room. But now he must learn that not every cry will bring someone running to him."

"Zoltán."

"Sit down, Ilona."

The tone convinced her. The crying continued, with pauses, which I was sure were left to listen for footsteps.

"You are a hard father," she said.

I looked up then. "You may be sure that I will not be that."

"Listen to that crying, the poor darling."

"When he sees that no one is coming, he will change his philosophy soon enough. You'll see."

She gazed down at her plate.

"How long must he cry before I will be allowed to help him?"

"If I thought he needed help, I would go myself. Now."

She sat without eating, but I took some food and said the blessing. In a few minutes, the crying became a whimper, and then momentary silence, and then gurgling.

"Now you may go and look in at him, but don't pick him up. Come right back."

Ilona stood and threw her napkin on the table. She was gone nearly a minute. She came back, snapped out her napkin and took some food.

"Did you pick him up?"

She took a mouthful of food.

"Did you?"

"No." She glared at me.

"Good," I said. "These potatoes are excellent."

*   *   *

Christmas Eve Ilona and I stayed at the orphanage. Nothing more had happened in the war between the Allies and the Axis powers. In fact, some of us had begun to call the conflict "The Phony War." It had been so long since the radio carried any news of fighting that we allowed our spirits to buoy a little and carry on the season.

Mrs. Vrabel, more softened by the arrival of Henrik than I had supposed possible, made cookies for the whole orphanage. Mrs. Greta stayed the night as well, and we sang and ate sweets and bade each other "Merry Christmas." I even started one song myself.

"Now boys," I said, "I know you want to sit up all night, but–"

"Wait," said Ilona. "We have a surprise for you."

"What?"

"Well, we can't tell you just yet. You have to wait a bit."

"How much did it cost?"

"Nothing but our silence."

I dropped my chin and looked up at her.

She gave the look back.

"So everyone here knows about it but me?"

The boys said together, "Yes!"

I picked Henrik up and held him before me. "Even you, son? How could you side against your Papa?"

He smiled and kicked his legs. The boys laughed.

Then came a rap at the door. Ilona jumped up.

"At last," she said.

She pulled back the door, and in with a gust of winter air came Bootblack, lugging a sack that bulged and banged against the doorjamb.

"Now," he said, "you can start Christmas!"

Boys came running and bounding from every corner and stormed the man. Even in the tumble, I saw that he was now a captain.

"All right! All right!" He pulled the sack up by the bottom and little boxes and bags spilled out in profusion. "One for everybody."

The chaos shifted to the floor. Bootblack grinned at me. "I left yours by the porch."

"Mine?"

He motioned toward the door with his head.

I went out. There in the light coming through the windows, at the bottom of the steps, stood a horse.

Suddenly Ilona was behind me with a coat, and Bootblack came out with a lantern. Children crowded the doorway and filled the windows.

"Merry Christmas," he said. "Courtesy of the Hungarian army."

Even in the lantern light, I could see it was a gray with regulation saddle and bridle.

"Are you serious?"

"I am. Officers in the cavalry ride horses. When I found out you were to have a horse, I wrote Ilona and told her I would bring it myself–for Christmas."

I had stepped down to the horse as he talked and taken the bridle.

"Hello, boy."

"His name is Alexander," said Bootblack.

Bootblack and I took him down to the army stables and put him up. I ran my hands over his thick coat. He was young, his muscles hard. I smacked him stoutly on the shoulder.

"I never thought I'd have a horse to call my own."

"He's not exactly yours," Bootblack said.

"Close enough," I said.

At the orphanage, Ilona had cleared most of the boys out to bed. Henrik slept soundly on his grandmother's shoulder. Dani had reappeared when we stomped in, talking too loudly for the hour.

We took off our coats and, belatedly, started to whisper.

"The boys must have a plan for where you are to sleep."

Bootblack nodded. "I suppose."

Dani was beside me then, waiting.

I leaned down. "Up late, aren't you?"

He said nothing, but pulled a small package in brown paper and string from behind his back.

"For me?"

His head went up and down, his eyes averted, as though he were being scolded.

I squatted down and undid the package. Inside was a pair of black socks, neatly and evenly done.

"Why, thank you, Dani. I've been so busy, I haven't had time to look after my own socks."

"They're not as big as a horse," he said.

"What would I do with socks as big as a horse?"

"I just wanted to give you something important."

I felt the socks with my thumb.

"A man can live the winter without a horse, son–but not very well without socks."

He smiled then and suddenly wrapped his arms around my neck.

"Merry Christmas, Zoli bacsi!"

"Merry Christmas, Dani."

* * *

"This building is full, Sergeant Galambos," the soldier said.

"Yes. I think we'll have to open the old fortress."

The men flung the bundles of heavy clothes and blankets back on the wagons. Alexander snorted and tossed his head, white frost rolling out his nose.

"Is the train car unloaded?"

"Not quite, sir."

"All right. What's left here and on the train bring to the fortress."

"Yes, sir."

I turned Alexander toward the fortress. Feri came over the bright snow toward me, waving a paper.

"Look! A telegram. I never knew anybody that got a telegram!"

I reined the horse in and bent to take the paper.

COMING THROUGH KOMAROM. STOP. MORNING TRAIN.
STOP. DECEMBER 30. STOP. PALI.

I said, "How about a ride, Feri?"

He had his foot in the stirrup before I even had mine all the way out. He swung on behind me and held on.

I nudged Alexander with my heel, and he sprang away with the vigor and grace of a Lipizzan. Feri laughed with pleasure. We bounded along the side of the road.

"Let's take the bridge," said Feri.

"We're going to the station," I called back.

"Let's take it anyway."

Alexander wheeled left and thundered over the planks of the bridge.

"Just like Horthy," Feri said.

Even with the detour, we were well ahead of the train. Alexander blew and stamped from the run. Feri slid off and stood on the packed snow around the platform.

"Thanks," he said.

"I'm meeting an old friend," I said. "Will you tell Mrs. Vrabel not to wait lunch?"

"Sure." And he was gone.

The train was late, which was to be expected that time of year. Then at last, it came, whistling through the cold, squealing on the tracks to stop. It snorted as it paused, like a winded horse, resting only to run on. As I waited, the excitement in me stilled and froze into apprehension.

A handsome man in a brushed wool coat filled the opening above the iron stairs. I looked for no small time before I knew it was Pali.

I tapped Alexander into a walk. Pali looked in my direction, and nodded at the uniform, and scanned the platform again.

"May I help you, sir?" I said.

"No, thanks, I'm waiting for someone."

"A friend?"

"Yes." He looked back when he spoke, taking down his hand from the pole and squaring his shoulders.

I took off my hat. "Maybe I know him," I said.

Pali leaned out from the railing, holding out his hand.

"Zoli, I didn't know you!"

I leaned over from Alexander and took his hand.

"I wasn't sure it was you, either. Are you staying?"

He shook his head. "I have to be on this train when it pulls out. I'm due back in Budapest tonight."

"Not Bratislava?"

"I'm going to the University in Budapest." He looked me up and down. "Sergeant, is it?"

"Mostly it's Zoli bacsi. At the orphanage." Alexander shifted his weight under me. "And I have a wife–and a son."

"I thought you had a married cast about you. Do I know her?"

"I don't think so–Ilona Vrabel."

"No." He adjusted the collar of his big coat.

"No wife for you yet?"

"Still free," he said. "Milike married last summer."

"She did? Who?"

"An official in Bratislava." His eyes were down, his voice light.

"You don't like him?"

"He's a Roman Catholic."

I felt this news like rain on the back of my neck.

Pali said, "He's older than she is quite a bit."

We wavered in a long silence. He looked away at the edge of Komárom. I brushed the mane of my horse all to one side.

"Pali, I'm sorry. I was wrong to accuse you."

"Your letter was enough," he said. "The past is past. Forgotten."

He turned his face to me, and his smile was the one I remembered from the other side of our long interim.

"I wish you could stay a while."

"So do I." He stepped over and knocked a little snow from the edge of the car with his foot. "I have such a feeling, Zoli, like being swallowed. If I can finish school before—before we go to war, too, I'm going to try for a position in the embassy."

"You'll make it," I said.

"God willing."

We stayed where we were, but our conversation brought us side by side again after that, and when in an hour or so, the train pulled out, I waved him off as long as I could see him. I knew that if it were ten years or twenty or not until glory that I saw him next, it would not be as long as it had been this time.

May, 1940

"The weather stays so cold and rainy," said Dani. "I can't get anything planted."

He held his index fingers out for Henrik, who grasped onto them as he waddled in from his trek from the sink.

"It's an awful spring," said Mrs. Vrabel.

We did not know then how encompassing her statement was, not until less than two weeks later, when the Netherlands and Belgium fell to Nazi Germany and we understood the silence had been only a lull and not the end.

Polish Jews who had escaped to Hungary began to come through Komárom to get to the West through Yugoslavia. Hundreds came on the trains, with but a bag or two in their hands, with drawn faces and eyes like winter stars.

Once I thought I saw Hevesi, and I ran after the man, but when I caught up to him, it was not Hevesi's face that turned to me with sudden shock.

"I'm sorry," I said. "I thought you were someone else."

He still regarded me as though he were judge and I were suspect.

I took some money from my pocket. "Please take this," I said. "If you don't need it, find someone who does."

He did not reach for it.

"Please, take it, on behalf of who I thought you were."

He took it then, and tipped his head, and went on.

It was only the end of June when France, one of the strongest nations in the world, drowned in the black tide, went under without hope, without a hand to hold to, and was gone.

The next morning after breakfast, I called the boys to silence, stood up, and prayed as though I alone besought Almighty God for Hungary. And when I finished, I looked out upon my boys with the knowledge that some would soon be old enough to draft, should that terrible necessity befall us.

Ilona came to the doorway of the hall. In my earnestness I had not heard the door or her going to answer it, she told me later. And in my astonishment, I barely saw her then, for behind her were Dezső and my mother.

Chapter Seven
Battle Weary

"Mama," I said before I could stop myself.

Every eye in the room was on her, and she was unmoved, standing with her dignity and regality still about her, but in exile now, her hair sweeping back iron-gray from her face, and her intent eyes on me.

I went down the length of the table and took Ilona's hand.

"Won't you come home with us?" I said to Mama.

She swept in the kitchen with a glance and then nodded to me.

Mrs. Vrabel had opened the back door and the boys were going out as though from church, subdued and contained.

"Hello, Dezső." I finally took my eyes away from the woman I had not expected to see again.

"Hello, Zoli."

"This is my wife, Ilona," I said, to both of them.

Dezső merely looked down, but my mother let a slightly softer look come in her eye and said, "Ilona."

"Mrs. Galambos. Dezső."

Margarette had directed Henrik toward us, and he came now, in his happy, paddling way, his arms up for balance. I scooped him up.

"And this is Zoltán Henrik."

My mother almost smiled, but she did not reach for him or regard him long.

"Please," I said, holding my hand out toward the front door, "our house is not far."

"I'm so glad you've come," said Ilona. "We have an extra room, Mrs. Galambos, and you'll be our first guest."

I could see that Ilona was moving us onto the floor in Henrik's room, and I found yet another reason to admire my wife.

"I won't be here tonight," my mother said.

"Oh," said Ilona.

We had gone down the steps. A wagon and horses went by in the street, and the rumble filled a moment.

My mother might have been an ambassador's wife, I thought, had the choices been different, for she had the presence and the bearing. She was momentarily ahead of me at the turning of the walkway, and she touched the collar of her dress, to be sure it laid flat in the back. Her hand trembled.

Ilona said, "Henrik was just a year old last March." She patted his round arm.

We crossed the street, just ahead of a truck. We took a lane between two houses that was lined with flowers.

"Zoltán," said Mama, "I want you to take Dezső."

I stopped. "Take Dezső?"

"Keep him with you."

Dezső fixed his eyes on Mama and did not look away.

I studied to find an answer. Ilona stood as quiet as the wall behind her. I could not follow the undercurrent I sensed in my mother.

"What has happened?"

My mother drew in a breath as if to speak, but no words came. She seemed bent in the middle, as though she would put her hand to a rail were it there.

Dezső turned his gaze to me. I had seen that same look before, but not from him.

"Victor died," he said.

My voice came out in a sound of sudden pain. Before I regained myself, my mother lifted her head.

"By his own hand," she said.

"Oh, Victor."

I felt Ilona's hand on my arm, and then she was taking Henrik. Dezső sagged, free now of the message that had so burdened him.

I held out my hand to my mother. She looked at it as though to take it would change her immeasurably. Then with a solemnity at once both graceful and lost, she took it.

"I'm sorry," I said.

She took her hand away and drew herself up.

In a moment more I said, "We should be at home."

The house was never more beautiful to me, its spareness lending serenity to the familiarity. My mother looked around, but I saw no judgment in her.

"What will you do?" I said.

"I have enough to live on," she said.

"Have you asked Dezső about coming here?"

"He is eleven. What would he say?"

I turned toward him. "Dezső, what do you say?"

"I want to stay with Mama."

I looked to Ilona. She sat against the windowsill with Henrik in her arms. Her face was clear and open; the decision was wholly mine.

"He is just afraid of change," Mama said. "It will be all right in a little while."

"No," said my brother. "I want to stay where I belong."

"And Béla?" I said.

"Béla is only a year and five months from joining the army."

"The army?"

"This is what he says he will do."

I felt more tired then than when I used to come in from the fields with Papa and Victor. A shudder ran over me to think of Victor walking beside me to turn the hay in the sun.

My mother looked tired too. I had seen her worn out with work and unhappiness, but this, this look carried in it the weariness of despair.

"You're tired," I said. "Would you like to lie down?"

I so expected her to refuse that I had not made a move.

"Yes," she said.

I showed her to the bedroom and pulled a pillow out from under the quilt.

"Thank you," she said, and waited for me to close the door.

Ilona was cutting bread and cheese for Dezső.

"What do you like best?" she was saying.

"History, I guess," he said.

I sat down beside him. "Dezső, tell me straight now, what do you want?"

"I don't know." He chewed the cheese slowly. "Mama needs me. She does, Zoli."

"What does Béla say?"

"Béla says you and Papa were right about things."

I looked at Ilona and back to my brother.

"Why didn't he come?"

"Hay to get in." He felt his pockets. "He sent this. Don't tell Mama." He handed over a note.

I turned it in my fingers.

"Do you want to stay a while and then decide?"

He chewed thoughtfully. "All right."

My mother would not be persuaded to stay. I walked with her to the train that evening. I had never been angry with her, and so the distance that was maintained came from her resolve, not mine.

She asked me about Henrik, whether he talked at all, whether he was always so cheerful. She said that he looked like her people. The station was just before us.

I rubbed my jaw. "I know you don't want to hear me on this, but there is no comfort in all the books you have like there is in the one I left with Papa."

"Don't, Zoltán. You and Béla are of a different mind. Leave it at that."

We were nearly to the platform. A whistle blew.

"Why did you bring Dezső to me then?"

She stepped up to get on the train. She put up her hand to find the strands of hair that had blown loose.

"Good-bye, Zoltán."

Her face was beautiful still, in spite of everything.

"Good-bye," I said. "Mama."

April, 1941

Dezső had lived with Ilona and me for a few weeks, and he and Dani found in each other ready friends. Dezső went home to visit Mama four or five times, and once I had permitted Dani to go with him. When they came back, Dezső asked to stay in the orphanage with the other boys, and I allowed it, for many reasons.

The best reason revealed itself that Christmas when Dani came to me and said that Dezső wanted to be a Christian. It was like the birth of Henrik to me, that conversation with those boys.

"Now your brother is my brother, too," said Dani. "I always wanted to have a brother."

"Well, that would make me your brother as well," I said.

He sat back in his chair and grinned. "No, you're Zoli bacsi."

The spring came, and with it, Germany's demand that we join its armies against Yugoslavia, despite the treaty we had with that country of eternal friendship. Premier Teleki and Regent Horthy refused. Horthy was practical, knowing too well the treachery of Hitler with all his other allies. Teleki was, above all, an honorable man; he refused because no Magyar would so disgrace himself as to betray a friend.

German troops came through Hungary anyway, helped–Bootblack told us–by Nazi infiltrators. We all had known that the Germans would come, permission or not. It was, then, in utter disbelief that we heard the news about Teleki.

I sat astride Alexander, overseeing a train car loaded with flour and rice. The private appeared before me, white-faced.

"What is it?"

"Premier Teleki, sir. He has taken his own life."

Dinner was not as quiet as I had expected. The magnitude of the loss had not seemed to reach the boys. I was angry with them, at their incapacity.

"Wasn't it noble?" said one young man.

I stood up, in the middle of the meal, the horror growing in me.

"No," I said. "There is nothing noble here. Only dreadful and wrong and irreversible. What has this done but rob a people poor already of their treasure? Isn't it more noble to fight those who made us break the treaty? God does not give us life to have it thrown away. No, Teleki should have stayed with us. I ask you–what is noble here?"

My voice trembled, and I felt like dismissing them from the table. They sat with their heads down.

"It will come to nothing. It will be the greater disgrace."

I sat down again. Ilona asked her mother to find some music on the radio. There was no more talking.

Late that night I lay awake thinking of Victor. The years behind closed in on me, and the tears rolled hot on my face. I thought also of the days ahead. With a surety, they were grim;

war for us was inevitable. But I could not have guessed how long in coming.

April, 1944

"A major to see you, sir."

I nodded and stood up. My desk was strewn with papers, by which I was trying to stretch short rations and medicine further than they would go.

The major was Bootblack.

I saluted the rank and took the hand of my friend.

"I think we can stop blaming the Gymnásium for these promotions now," I said. "You must be a good officer."

He wagged his head. "Always in the right place at the wrong time. How's Ilona–and Henrik?"

"They're well. Henrik has a brother since you were here last."

His eyes widened. "Tell me."

"Kalman. After Ilona's father. He's six months old."

He shook my hand again. Then he sat down, and I followed his lead. His face had the lines of command growing in it, but there was yet about his mouth something of the Bootblack of the train days.

"Sometimes," he said, "I wish we could go to the old tree, all of us, and pray together and worry about nothing more than Kovaly's Latin tests."

I nodded. His face seemed thinner, but then all our faces did. And the darkness under his eyes told me more than any field report. I waited for the rest.

He passed his hand over his mouth and then dropped his hands, gripping his knees.

"I am here officially to order your captain to Budapest, which I have done. And to order you to take the reserves out of Komárom immediately."

"It's over then."

"The Germans are retreating. The Russians are advancing to liberate us. They will occupy Hungary within the week."

"Where do we go?"

"Try to get the supply unit west to Austria or Germany. Take what supplies you can. Don't leave anything for the Russians. Burn stuff, if you have to."

"Do you think we can't get there? You say 'try.' "

He took his hat from under his arm. "All the markers and town names are taken down. It's easy to get lost."

"How long do I have to move out?"

"Three days. Advise the citizens to get out as well. But you can't take the time to force them."

He was standing again.

"Can I take Ilona with me?"

"Your privilege, Zoli. Do what you think best there. Move at night as much as you can. The Russian airplanes are always overhead."

"All right."

"And, if you are taken," he said, and paused as though weary, "pray the Lord they are the Americans."

We faced each other across the desk, Bootblack looking at me as if to memorize my face. We shook hands, as we had on the train the day we graduated from the Gymnásium, but this time with men's responsibilities, not boyish dreams, pulling us apart.

"Go with God, Zoltán."

"And you, my friend."

* * *

Ilona's face was white. She held Kalman asleep in her arms. Henrik ran up the stairs and called down to her.

"Mama, I'm coming down the mountain again. Are you ready?"

She did not answer him.

"Henrik," I said, "come sit down."

He came and stood by his mother. I motioned with my head, and he sat down on the floor. Dezső came into the hall then.

"You sent for me?"

"I have to evacuate the city. Starting now. I'm taking Ilona and the boys with me in the supply unit. Do you want to go with us or go back to Szilas?"

He was tall for fourteen and filled out. He looked like our mother, a handsome face with sharp eyes.

"What's happened?"

"The Russians are coming from the north against the German forces."

"Then I need to go take care of Mama."

I looked at the brother who only moments before had been a child. I embraced him. "That was a man's answer."

I kept my hand on his shoulder.

"You had better leave tonight or in the morning. As soon as I announce this, the trains will be full."

He took a long breath. Then he was gone up the stairs.

Ilona still had said nothing. She watched me with a hunted look.

"I have to get the other boys away from here," I said.

"How?" she said at last.

I didn't know. "Are you all right?"

She nodded slowly. "What about Mama?" Her eyes grew large and round. "And Editke and Margarette?"

I put my hand to my head. "Ask your mother what she wants to do. Then get all the boys together. I'll be back as soon as I can."

The telephone in the army office was ringing when I got there. The sergeant in Kassa wanted to know what I had heard. He had no orders yet. As soon as I hung up, I telephoned Toth.

It took some time to get him to the telephone from his house, but at last he was there.

"I'll be there in the morning," he said. "I'm leaving now."

Pataki, my assistant, had Alexander saddled and waiting.

"Good man," I said as I swung into the saddle. "Sound assembly."

The men came instantly, row on row. I hollered to them.

"Fill every available wagon and cart with stuff from the fortress and the other buildings. When every movable conveyance is full, report back here."

I wheeled Alexander toward the orphanage.

The boys were there, waiting with sober faces. Several had already left to join the army. But twenty-one were still in my charge, still looking to me for help.

"We have to evacuate the city," I told them. "I have to go with the army. But Pastor Toth will be here in the morning to take you with him or find you a place to stay."

A little boy, about eight, put his head on his knees and sobbed. Ilona went to sit beside him and stroked his hair.

"Any of you who are sixteen," I hesitated and then went on, "can do what you will."

"Can't we go with you, Zoli bacsi?" said Dani.

I shook my head. "I'm sorry. I can't take you."

He looked as though he might cry as well.

"I love you, boys. But God loves you more. And I must trust Him to look after you. I want you to trust Him too."

They still looked at me, hoping that I could change my mind.

"Get your things together. Be good soldiers for me."

It was daybreak before the wagons were loaded, canvassed, and strapped. I rode the lines, checking every detail, making sure there was a fair selection of all goods–flour, rice, sugar, salt, pepper, paprika, salted bacon, smoked sausage, blankets, coats, and boots. Several wagons carried only grain for feed.

"What's left?" I asked.

"Nearly twice what's here, sir."

I rode back to the front.

"Fall in."

The tired men formed their lines.

"Now, I want every man here to get everything he wants for his family—no one else—just his family. Do that in two hours. After that, I will let the townspeople take the rest. Dismissed."

There was a roar of approval, and the men broke for the storehouses.

Pataki said, "Begging your pardon, sir, is that regulation?"

I looked down at his bright eyes and his red mustache.

"I suppose you have read the regulation book on this?"

"Yes, sir. It says to burn everything you cannot carry."

"Yes. Well, whoever wrote that didn't have starving neighbors and half-clothed children on every hand. If we must burn something, Pataki, let it be the regulation book."

"Yes, sir!"

"Now, would you please collect for me from the storehouse—and remember my mother-in-law."

"I do remember her, sir."

The stubble on my face reminded me I had been up since five the day before. Ilona and Mrs. Vrabel had managed the orphanage on their own. Seventeen boys were ready with their small bundles, sitting on the stairs, their quietness telling on them.

Ilona came to me as I entered. "Feri, Wass, and the Iren brothers already left," she said. She drew near my ear. "Dani won't talk to me."

I felt a weight in my chest. "What about your mother?"

"She says she's staying here. There's no talking to her. She telegrammed the girls to stay in Leva."

"All right. I think she should stay in our house. This place is sure to be taken for a barracks."

She leaned her head into my shoulder.

"I'm having Pataki stock the cellar with supplies to last a year. And stuff to trade–Ilona?"

"I hear, Zoli. I'm just so frightened."

"We'll be all right," I said, and I wished I believed it.

I studied the boys' faces, so grim and distant already. I thought of the Jews who had come on the trains. I suddenly thought of Béla, wherever he was by now. I held Ilona for a minute more.

"Dani," I said, "could I see you?"

He came to me. I led him to the kitchen and sat him down. Ilona followed, her eyes welling.

"Son, if I could take you with me, I would."

He just stared down.

"It's all right," he said.

"Dani, look at me."

He worked his mouth and then brought his head up with courage.

"I want to ask you something, and you are free to answer any way you want. Understand?"

He said, weakly, "Yes."

"Mrs. Vrabel is staying here, in my house. Would you be willing to stay with her? She talks tough, but she needs help, I think."

His whole self brightened. "Oh, yes. I could do that for you, Zoli bacsi. I'll take good care of her."

"Thank you."

Ilona was crying now, leaning on the wall with her hand over her mouth. I touched her cheek.

"I have one more thing to see to," I said. "Papa Kovaly might need some help."

*   *   *

"Where are we?" Henrik asked.

He sat in the front of the covered wagon with Pataki. I did not like to see his face getting dark with lack of play.

I reined Alexander near.

"Somewhere west of Bratislava, I think," I said.

I looked at Pataki, and Henrik nodded as though he were an old man pondering the answer.

We made such little headway, traveling slowly in the dark, hiding in the woods all day. Two months of this dodging, and still no Hungarian fighting units had appeared.

I pulled back the flap to see my wife and other son. Ilona lay half-reclined on the generous pile of blankets Pataki had gotten. In the dimness, she seemed to look serene, as though the wagon cover were the walls of an embassy. Kalman sat on her lap. She smiled at me.

I held Alexander in and let the next wagon come abreast of me.

The driver said, "Yes, sir?"

"I'm going to take a blanket off the wagon and ride to that farm over there and see if I can make a trade for our breakfast."

He nodded.

"Keep moving. I'll catch up with you."

The farmer's wife gladly parted with some eggs and milk for the heavy wool blanket. But it hardly would feed twenty-seven men and my family. But it was the best deal I could make. I rode back toward the unit, holding the bag of eggs. They were wrapped in newspaper, but I took no chances.

There was another farmhouse in the distance. I could still see the wagons to the left. I turned Alexander to the house. A stout woman there looked me up and down.

"What do I want with eggs?" she said. "I have chickens myself."

I fought down my Hungarian officer's pride. "Please," I said, "I have children with me."

"No soldier has children with him."

"If I bring my son here, will you believe me?"

"I might."

I looked at the sky. The sun was nearly full up.

Pataki took the eggs gingerly, and then the milk. I reached for Henrik, and he came flying. He took his place in front of me and grabbed into the mane.

"Let's go, Papa."

It took only a small opening, and his playfulness was upon him again, undiminished.

"Pull off in that woods over there," I told Pataki. "We won't be long."

Alexander snorted to a halt in the farmyard. The woman leaned out the window.

"Well, I'll be," she said.

"Hello," said Henrik.

His blond hair shone in the early sun.

"Hello yourself."

He laughed. "Papa and I rode over from the wagon. Alexander is one good horse."

It still jolted me to hear my words come out his mouth.

She came out of the house then and up to Henrik. She rubbed a smudge from his face with her thumb.

"Was I dirty?" he said.

She looked at me. "I might have some extra around here," she said.

She returned with a sack full of bread and vegetables and cheese.

I offered her money.

"What good does that do anybody? Just see this little one gets out of this."

I urged Alexander to a gallop. And I decided that Henrik would ride with me on all my begging trips.

*   *   *

The wagons began to show some signs of having traveled rough roads at night for months. Instead of sleeping in shifts during the day, we now began to trade off carpentry duty as well.

Ilona cooked every morning that I could find something. We built the fire so that the smoke would be gone before the light was distinct and after the true darkness had passed, so that neither smoke nor flame would draw attention.

Some days I could not find enough for both of us, and on such occasions I would break a small bite from whatever I brought her and swallow it before I got to her.

"Aren't you eating?" she would say.

"I ate mine on the way in," I would answer.

By October, we were exhausted, almost beyond repair at times, and yet we had never seen or even heard a battle or come upon any soldiers. For more than a week I had not even found a farm.

The horses were wearing out, and the dried meats, for all my careful rationing and stretching with bartered and begged food, were nearly gone. We ate less and less, until our clothes began to hang on us. I went on every evening with fewer options.

Henrik sat quietly without being told, and his chatter to Pataki dwindled. Ilona never questioned me, not even with her eyes, but she seldom laughed. When I sat by her in the firelight, I saw that her hair was dull and her fair skin sallow.

She took her place under my arm and put her face against my neck.

"I love you, Zoli."

I put my chin on her head and watched the fire until it died out.

I went out, away from camp, and fell on my face.

"Dear God, I am at my wit's end. My wife, my children–I can't–they are going to starve, Lord. My heart is breaking. I need to know what I should do. Please. Please."

There was only the call of birds of the woods and the smell of earth for answer.

In the evening, I motioned the wagons out, with hope that faded with the lowering sun. We lumbered along, the wheels dipping into potholes and jangling our goods, and our nerves.

The night had no moon. It seemed so long and dark as to be the last night of the world. But the sky thinned with light again, and the sunrise came, as it had since creation, but somehow it surprised me this time.

And then Pataki said, "Sergeant, what's there?"

Ahead the silhouettes of soldiers and trucks bobbed on the crest of a hill.

My heart pounded in my throat.

"I pray to God they are Americans," I said.

Chapter Eight
Toward Home

It was no use to run now. The soldiers had come over the little rise and were upon us.

I held up my hand to stop the caravan behind me.

The silhouettes on the crest slowed, and then a contingent of about ten mounted soldiers came riding down to us. The sun was half up, but not enough to show me uniform insignia.

"Get in the wagon, Henrik."

He slipped under the flap. Pataki looked sideways at me and ran his finger across his lip.

"Stay calm," I called out.

The officer of the ten riders came in first. With relief that almost made me dizzy in the saddle, I saw his United States uniform.

He stopped a little distance from me. We sat on our horses and looked at each other.

"Who are you?" he said in German.

I spoke very little German. I gave him my name.

He said something else. I shook my head.

"No German," I said in Hungarian.

He pulled up his shoulders with a sigh.

"I speak English. Small English," I said.

His face changed. "What unit is this?"

"We are–" My English had not included military terms. I fought for a word.

"I speak Slovak," he said.

"Ah, so do I. We are only a supply unit. We carry grain and some clothes. I have my wife and children with me, by permission of the Hungarian government."

He looked very clean to me and polished. My own boots I knew were hardly recognizable as boots any more. His eyes were direct; I liked him.

"Really? You are not a fighting unit?"

I said, "My wife, sir." Then I called to Ilona in Hungarian.

She came through the flap with Kalman in one arm and Henrik under the other.

The officer smiled. "What about the other wagons?"

"Search them," I said.

He spoke to the man beside him, and the man took three soldiers and rode back the line.

"Where are we?" I asked.

"Austria," he said.

I rubbed the back of my neck.

The soldiers returned, satisfied that I was telling the truth.

The American officer adjusted his position in his saddle, and I could tell that he was thinking. Then he asked me to get down, and as I did, he did.

The sun had risen fully. The morning was crisp and the sky already brilliant blue. The officer drew a map from his saddlebag and laid it out on the wagon seat. Pataki got off and stood by the horses. Ilona pulled Henrik back into the wagon.

From inside he said, "But Mama, I want to see the paper. Who is that shiny man?"

The officer pointed to the map. "We have advanced to here. If you stay behind this line, you'll be all right. But don't get out of this area. Don't try to go home."

"You are not taking us prisoners?"

He shook his head. "I'm handling you like escaping civilians."

"What's happening in Hungary? Do you know?"

"No, the Russians are advancing from the east." He folded the map. Then he put his hand on the rump of the wagon horse and patted the animal. "I do know that the Germans have arrested your president–Horthy."

*   *   *

Our unit was broken up, and we went on our own to find a place to stay and something to eat. The men, I was sure, could spread out and find work and shelter in the farms around. I took the wagon, and Alexander, and left the other wagons and horses to the men. We divided what small goods were left.

Pataki gave his blanket to Ilona.

"For Kalman," he said. "When winter comes."

I chose a direction and headed the wagon in it. At least we could travel in the daylight now. Henrik revived in the light, and his little voice came more and more into my ear. At home, his questions might have wearied me, but here, they swirled around me like summer birds after the rain.

I prayed as I drove Alexander, and I prayed as I unhitched him, and I prayed when we ate, and I prayed when we didn't.

In three days, we came to the edge of a farm. As we drew closer, the buildings took on a more and more deserted air. The weeds had grown up by the house. The barn was silent.

"Isn't anybody home?" Henrik said.

"Well," I said, "we might be. For a little while."

We moved into the house, although the wagon seemed sturdier. There was no furniture, except a broken chair and, of all things, a cradle. We took straw from the barn and made beds on the floor with our blankets. I set two empty barrels by the fireplace with a board over them, and we had a bench and a table, alternately.

Behind the house I sat down, drawn to the stream rolling by. The water was swift and dark, with banks that hung over the stream like dank awnings. From time to time, a trout slipped out from under the close cover of the banks and darted for an insect, and then slid back into hiding.

Several times the fish appeared and disappeared, and I rose and stepped down into the stream. The current pressed against my legs, as though to turn me from my purpose, to argue with the absurdity of the plan.

I put my hands under the bank, palms up, and moved them along slowly, back and forth, walking sideways, always slowly, waiting. At last my right hand brushed against the slippery underside of a trout. The fish stayed still, and I brought my other hand under it too. Then in one quick move, I raised my hands and pinned the trout under the top of the bank.

It thrashed and flailed, but I got my thumb into its mouth and brought it out of the water. The sun flashed on its speckled sides.

Ilona cooked it, and we shared it on the grand dining room table.

"It might have been easier," I said to Ilona, "to be American prisoners. We would surely have eaten better."

"We're fine," she said. "We're all together, and we're out of the fighting."

"Papa," said Henrik, "when can we go home?"

"Soon, I think."

But the Germans were more tenacious than I thought, than anyone had thought. We were there for the winter. I found a neighbor by the smoke from his chimney, a miller, with whom I found no common tongue, but with whom I traded Alexander for a good cow. We milked the cow for a time, and then butchered it and jerked the meat.

The miller took me with him to a small village when he went, and I traded some of the jerked meat for dried apples and lard to cook with and some potatoes. Even in the dark poverty of my childhood I had never been so near to having nothing.

A chilly morning late in the fall, I foraged the woods, hoping it might yield up some food I had overlooked somehow. It seemed I smelled ham. I ran my hand across my face, to clear the imagination. Then I heard talking, shouting rather, and I scouted on.

The soldiers were in American uniforms, but there were only three or four. The smell of ham hung in the air, and my stomach growled. After a moment in the cover of the brush, I came forward into the yard of the camp. The soldiers looked up, one stood up, but they did not stop me.

I made a motion of scooping food toward my mouth and ducked my head to them. They looked at each other. Then one called out, to the tents behind him.

"Jack!"

Another man, aproned and greasy, came through the flap and grinned at me. He waved me in, and I went. I thought briefly that I had fallen into a stupor from hunger and was dreaming this abundance of food. Pancakes and coffee from breakfast still sat on the makeshift counter, and the provisions of lunch were heaped up on the tables.

I helped this cook with the big pots and pared potatoes and ate the ham and beans he offered. I pointed to the pancakes.

"Please? For my wife?"

He said something I did not understand and emptied a gallon preserve container. He fixed a wire handle to it and held it out.

"Take what you need," I heard, and I did–that day and every day through the winter.

On this provision my family lived until the spring returned and gave us berries and wild fruit and a little hope for the end of war and wandering.

September, 1945

"Papa, someone is riding in," said Henrik. He danced around in a circle, clapping.

It was the miller, and behind him was a low wagon. I went out to meet them, and Henrik came along.

The driver of the wagon was black, and he wore a red cross on his armband. He smiled hugely.

He said, in Czech, "I've come to take you home. This man says you are a Hungarian. From which part?"

"From Czechoslovakia," I said.

He said, "Then you are among the winners."

"The war is over?" I said.

"Yes. Hitler is dead. Germany is defeated."

The scourge was lifted, but I felt only weariness.

"We don't have much to collect," I said.

"That's all right," he said. "Our trucks are just a little way out. We have time."

I became aware suddenly that Henrik was stone still. The driver looked from me to the boy.

Then he pulled something from the sack beside him on the seat and held it out to Henrik. I could tell, although I had never seen such a thing, that it was American candy.

Henrik looked up at me, and I nodded. He stepped forward and took it quickly and ducked back in beside me. He unwrapped it immediately, and when he saw what it was, he made big eyes.

"Oh, Papa," he said, "it's a sweet, isn't it?"

"It's chocolate," I said.

He cast a glance at his benefactor.

"Is he the chocolate man?"

I laughed, as loud as ever I had in my life. I told the driver, and he laughed, and he told the miller, and he laughed, until Ilona came out with Kalman to see what was the matter. Henrik only smiled and bit into the candy.

* * *

Komárom was not the city we remembered. Many buildings stood in charred and jagged remnants; windows were broken; German tanks still sat in the streets, broken down and detested.

Our house was untouched. Mrs. Vrabel stood in the kitchen, peeling apples. She was bent over her work and did not turn when the door opened.

"Dani," she said, "did you find any lard?"

"It's us, Mama," Ilona said.

Mrs. Vrabel raised her head, and she slowly backed away from the sink. The tears sprang from her eyes. She engulfed us all somehow in a great hug and sobbed.

She pulled away and wiped her face with her apron.

"I thought you weren't coming," she said.

She took Kalman and Henrik to her lap and kissed them over and over.

Dani came in with a cup of lard and dropped it.

He ran to me and held onto me.

"I never gave up hope," he said. "Never, never."

We ate together once again, laughing and crying and talking, such a hubbub. And I cannot remember what it was we ate.

The orphanage had no windows left. The doors were off the hinges. The floors were covered with trash. It smelled like an outhouse.

"Nazi swine," I said to Kovaly.

He shook his head. "This is the work of our Russian liberators."

His words went over me like cold rain.

"It'll take some doing to put this place to rights again."

Kovaly said, "Maybe you shouldn't."

"What? Why not? Because we are in Czechoslovakia again?"

He shook his head.

"I've been watching things," he said. "Maybe you and Ilona should get out–go to the West."

"No," I said. "This is only temporary. Things can be fixed."

"Not everything, I think," he said.

He moved a piece of broken glass with the toe of his shoe.

We had a letter from Dezső. Szilas had not suffered directly from the German occupation, but it had been looted by the Russians at the end of the war. Mama still had her house, but little else. Béla, it told us offhandedly, had come home with a wife.

"Keep praying for Mama," the letter ended. "I do."

Spring, 1947

Although Hungary had been forced by Germany to fight the Allies, we still were as much a part of the conquered enemy as the rest.

Ilona read the paper to me as I shelved the few books I had been able to buy for the store.

"The Paris Peace Conference has restored the boundaries established in the Treaty of Trianon. Furthermore, Hungary is charged to pay reparations to the Soviet Union."

I stood up and looked at the broken door that once lead to our back room. I made only the most necessary repairs.

"Reparations. That's a good one. And what are we to pay with–when the Russians carried off everything of value when we were 'liberated'?"

Dani handed me the hammer and picked up the nails he had straightened.

A Slovak officer appeared in the doorway.

"Galambos?"

"Yes?"

He thrust forth a paper.

"What's this?" I said.

"You have been appointed to represent the Hungarians in Slovakia who are being transported back here."

I stared at him. Ilona came up behind me and put her arm in mine.

"What does that mean?"

"The trade," he said, as though to a stupid child. "The population exchange. Hungarians–for Slovaks living in Hungary."

"Ah," I said, "yes."

"Report to Bratislava next week. It's in the document."

He left as he had come, like a rat, darting to the edge of its hole and then turning back on itself when the light hits it.

"How did that come about?" Dani said.

"I don't know. Probably my army connections. But maybe there will be a little money involved, eh?"

Ilona did not say anything, but I knew that she was afraid to have me leave.

The next day, Gab came home. I went to work on the orphanage early, and there he sat on the steps, and for a second, I felt as though I were coming back from the church to give the boys their afternoon lessons.

He stood up slowly, like a man who has seen much, and then some. He smiled at me, and in that look I saw the years that had gone by and the more lasting and subtle losses of war.

I went to him and embraced him. We shook hands for a long time.

"Gab, I'm so glad you came home."

"Just look at this," he said. "It's like this everywhere still." He sighed. "You should see Budapest. The Russians have smashed all the old statues and burned the churches. When I went there, it was the most wonderful place in the world. Now–"

He just looked away.

"How are you?" I said.

He nodded. "I came to tell you something, Zoli."

"Yes?"

"There's a resistance movement–"

"Yes, I know. Kovaly talks about it all the time. Are you–"

"Some of the leaders were arrested in Budapest last week."

I had a sudden charge in the center of my soul, but I could not tell from what cause.

"Major Nandor was among them."

"Bootblack."

My breath came hard, and I closed my eyes. That was it, what I had known, and not known. Death was easier to hear of; I could hardly keep from crying out. I wanted to break everything that stood for Russia into pieces with my bare hands.

"What's to be done?"

"We're trying to find out where they are." He looked into me. "I just thought you should know."

I did not work that day. I went to Kovaly.

He opened the door and read my face. He stepped back and let me in. We prayed for Bootblack and for Hungary and for ourselves. I left in the evening, comforted somewhat, but still with the empty feeling of a man who can do nothing visible and physical to change things.

"Zoltán, do you know whether Pali is in the embassy? If he is–"

"I'll write tonight."

"Be careful how you word things. Mail is read. Especially there, I'm sure."

* * *

I saw little in Bratislava that looked familiar. The general shape of the buildings seemed the same, but the essence of the place was gone. There was none of the graciousness, none of the warmth I had always found there.

Slovak and Russian soldiers haunted every corner. Hungarians walked among them, not smiling, not calling out to each other or even putting up a hand to wave.

Even had I known Milike's married name, I would not have tried to find her, but I did think of her and wonder whether she had found what she had looked for.

I returned the next day on the train, with my documents signed, the agreement in my hand. It guaranteed the Hungarian people the right to all their own property. And the government had given me the authority to hire workers to help load train cars. I thought of my brothers–they could use the money, and they knew how to work.

The streets of Komárom looked bright to me. The flowers were coming on. During the war I had always been struck with how the flowers came back, year after year, undaunted, unaffected.

"Hello," I called to a man who had been on the supply unit with me. He waved briefly.

I went home to change into my work clothes. My wife was there, just sitting at the table, her face white.

"Ilona. Why aren't you at the store?"

She looked up at me in such a way to make my heart stop. I turned to see if Kalman and Henrik were all right.

"What? What's happened?"

Ilona shook with gasps and started to cry. I held her against me, her racking sobs jerking us both.

"Tell me. Please."

She regained herself, drawing back from me just enough to speak, her forehead still on my shoulder.

"Slovak soldiers threw me out of the store yesterday. The Slovak city officials put a seal on the door."

Her tears came again. Mrs. Vrabel stood in the door of the kitchen, watching, her eyes dark and tired. Ilona breathed easier.

"Are you hurt?" I said.

She shook her head.

"They said the store is not ours. They said we dare not break the seal."

I brought her to me again until she cried no more. Then I wiped her face with my hand.

"Come," I said, "let's go see."

The seal was fixed to the door, as she had said, a proud and flimsy seal. I ripped it off and opened the door.

"Zoli!"

Ilona pulled back on my hand.

"What are you doing?"

"Opening the shop. It's way past time."

"Zoli! Please!"

I made her come into the store. She half-stumbled in, her eyes wide.

"Now," I said, "business as usual."

Her hands trembled, but she rolled up the shades and set out her cash box.

The police did not come back; neither did the city officials. We sold three books that day, and I considered it a good day. I knew that as soon as the word got around that I was running a resistance store, sales would go up.

At five o'clock I said, "Now, Ilona. Now we can close the shop."

Ilona locked the door, and we walked home. Mrs. Vrabel had supper waiting. Henrik met us at the door, still full of questions, but a nine-year-old's questions now.

"What will you do if the police come?"

"Ask them to leave," I said.

Mrs. Vrabel radiated disapproval.

"Are we having pie?" Kalman wanted to know.

Ilona picked him up and plunked him on the bench beside Henrik.

"No," she said. "No pie."

The door opened. A man came through the doorway and walked into our house as though it were a train station or a common business.

"What do you mean, taking the seal off my store?" he said.

I rose and met him before he reached the kitchen.

"Who are you?" I stepped into him, and he backed up. "You haven't introduced yourself."

He gave his name, a Slovakian name.

"I don't know how they do things in Slovakia, but in Hungary, a man knocks before he enters."

He dropped his gaze from mine. "I'm sorry," he said.

"All right. I accept. Now that I see you are a gentleman after all, won't you have coffee with us?"

He turned red and looked at the women and children he had frightened.

"Well," he said, "thank you."

Ilona made a place at the table, and her mother brought in another cup. Henrik moved over, missing nothing.

"Let's talk about your problem, shall we?" I said. "You don't understand what the problem even is, do you?"

He looked at me blankly. I nodded to Ilona, and she poured the coffee.

"First, let me show you something."

I went and got the papers I had signed years earlier for Kalocsai that made me the straw man owner of the shop—and the paper I had just brought down from Bratislava.

"This is the deed to the shop. Do you have such a paper?"

He shook his head. I held the other document up.

"This paper between your government and mine was signed just yesterday. See what it says? 'All Hungarian people are entitled to have and to move their own property.' "

He squinted at the paper.

"Now it seems to me that your problem is not with me. It's with the Slovak government officials. They tried to steal my store and give it to you."

He nodded, as a child does in school who almost but not entirely comprehends the lesson. He glanced around the table over the rim of the cup he held to his lips.

"What should I do?"

"I'm not the one to tell you what to do. But if my government had tried that on me, I would say, 'You city people have given me someone else's store, which is stealing. You promised me a shop. Now get me a real one.' "

He pondered this idea, swirling the last of his coffee in the cup. He set down the cup with a tiny clink against the saucer.

"I am sorry," he said. He rose to leave.

"That's all right," I said. "If you need any books or paper, we'd be happy to help you."

He put on his hat, nodded to us all, and left.

There was a silence, and then Henrik started to laugh. And soon we were all laughing. But later, deep in the night, I began to understand what Kovaly had been telling me: there was nothing to laugh at any more.

*   *   *

"This is right," said Kovaly. "There is nothing here for you, nothing here for your sons." His eyes were full of tears, but he smiled.

"I've had word from Pali. He doesn't know anything about Bootblack yet." I put my hand over my eyes and rubbed them, but the pain in my head stayed.

"You can't help him by staying, Zoltán. Better you should get your sons out–Bootblack may have died giving you and others the chance."

His cheeks were wet. I could not look at him.

"Gab told me where the weak spots are on the border of Austria. Where the new soldiers are, that aren't as slick yet. And he told me we should go like we're going on a picnic. Take nothing."

"Sure," said Kovaly.

I looked to him then with all the pleading I could muster.

"Won't you come with us?"

The look he gave me then was the look of a man who in better wisdom must refuse what his heart would grant.

He got up and took me in his arms as I was seated there and rocked me back and forth like a little, little child.

"You are such a son to me," he said.

After that we sat across from each other without speaking at all for a long while.

"I have to ask you," I said, "if you can, to do something."

He nodded.

"Can you, after we're gone a while, get the deed for the store to my mother?"

"Of course I will."

Then, when I had no more time and had borrowed against what little was left even then, I stood up.

"I will never know about Bootblack."

"I'll let you know. Somehow." His eyes were still so blue.

"But how can you? Every piece of mail is opened and read–and changed."

"I'll find a way," he said. "It will be my last gift to you–to find a way."

I embraced him once more.

"Good-bye, Papa."

He did not answer for some seconds.

"Go with God, son."

I left him the deed to the store. I laid it on the desk and walked out of his house without looking back.

Ilona had the basket ready, full of food, enough for ten.

"Papa," said Kalman, "are we going out?"

I picked him up and put him on my lap. His face was fair like his mother's, and his eyes were far older than his four years.

"Yes. We're going to have a picnic in the country. What do you think of that?"

"Good!" he said. "What will we eat?"

"Oh, we'll have roast pork and pudding and cookies."

I looked around at Henrik and Dani and Mrs. Vrabel.

"Who wants to go on the picnic with us?"

"I do, Papa," said Henrik.

"You remember what I told you about the picnic?"

He nodded.

Dani said, "I'd like to have some of that roast."

I felt my heart swell. "Good."

Mrs. Vrabel only shook her head. Ilona took her mother's hand. She bit her lip to hold in the crying. A few tears slipped away from her still, and she left the room.

I felt my pocket for the tickets to Sopron, a little town near the border of Austria. I saw that my briefcase was by the door. It held my Bible and my English/Hungarian dictionary and my diploma from the Gymnásium.

"Well, we must go. We can't be late for the picnic."

Kalman jumped down.

"Let's go! Let's go!"

Ilona returned, her face washed, but pale and sober. She quickly kissed her mother, held her face a moment—and then ran out to the street.

Mrs. Vrabel kissed Henrik and Kalman as though they would be gone just the afternoon. Never had I been more glad of her strength.

"Be good boys," she told them.

I took Mrs. Vrabel's hand.

"Take care of the house," I said.

"Zoltán."

I waited.

"I trust you with them all."

I hardly knew what to say. I could not find a name for the emotion that took me over. I kissed her.

She pushed me away. "Go. You have a long way to go."

We went away from our house, dressed in work clothes, carrying only a basket and a briefcase. I dared not look back. I felt that I was walking into the ocean.

I closed the door to our compartment on the train.

"When will we be there, Papa?" Kalman stood looking up at me, his head tipped back parallel with the floor.

"Pretty soon."

Ilona had not spoken since I had told her to pack the basket that morning.

Dani said, "Kalman, can you teach me that song Professor Kovaly sings to you?"

Kalman turned on his heels and faced Dani.

"Oh, come a blustery wind, my friend," he bellowed, his child's voice carrying the tune so well that I marveled he was my son.

The train whistle blew. Ilona's eyes welled with tears, but the tears did not fall.

Soon we were moving, in a steady rumbling wave over the tracks. It made me think of all the times I had waited for the train to carry me to Komárom, to take me to someplace far away.

Kalman finished his song.

"How's that?"

I heard a door slide open hard in a cubicle down from us in our car. Dani heard it too.

"Kalman," I said, "sing Papa another song."

In a minute, another door slid open with a bang, closer this time.

"Let's all sing," I said. "Drown me out though. You know how bad I am."

Our door slid open, and two Hungarian policemen with rifles and bayonets filled the opening.

Kalman stopped singing. "Hello."

The men said nothing. Kalman got out of Dani's lap and went to the door. Ilona only looked out the window at the trees flashing by. My heart banged against my ribs so that I thought they would break.

"Do you know what?" Kalman said.

Still the men said nothing. The one in front looked from Kalman to me and back to Kalman.

"We're going to a pig roast. I get to have cookies!"

The younger man smiled.

The other said, "Will you bring me something back?"

"Yes, sir, if there are any leftovers."

The man swept his gaze over us and stepped back, closing the door.

I took a deep breath. Ilona closed her eyes and leaned her forehead against the window.

Kalman said, "Come on, Papa. Sing with me."

It was raining in Sopron and getting dark. I collected the basket and the case.

"Are we there? How long till we eat, Papa?"

"Only a little farther, Kalman."

We walked away from the station. To the west were the cornfields Gab had said would show us the way. They appeared to be half a mile off.

"Oh," said Kalman. "It's raining on our picnic."

"No matter," I said. "There's some pines. We'll eat there."

Ilona spread the cloth and laid out the food. Dani helped her, but he kept looking to me, as though I should say or do something to make the event move faster.

Kalman ate heartily, especially his grandmother's cookies. He did not seem to notice we were not as hungry, that his mother ate nothing at all.

The clouds were deeper, darker. A little thunder rumbled somewhere. I stood up and dusted my pants, as though it mattered that there were crumbs. Ilona folded the cloth and laid it in the basket.

I said, "Leave the basket, Ilona."

She lowered it to the ground, slowly, as though she set down all of Hungary with it.

"Now we'll have a look at that corn over there, shall we? Let's stay together," I said. "But there's no hurry."

Henrik said, "Shouldn't the corn be in by now?"

"Some farmers leave the corn standing," I said. "They have a different harvest to get in."

Ilona glanced at me and held out her hand. I took it and kissed it. And we began, then, the walk of our lives.

The ground between us and the fields was open. I was sure we could be seen from the train station. We walked as though we might be going back to the house when our picnic had been rained out.

When the corn rustled around us at last, I gathered them all to me.

"I love you," I said to them. "Remember that."

We started down the rows, planted so as to lead those who dared to freedom.

"Just keep walking straight down the corn rows. Follow the row, Henrik."

I picked Kalman up and carried him.

The lifeless stalks rattled in the rain and with our passing. The darkness deepened, for the field was uncommonly long, and we could not go fast. The searchlights from the towers at the end of the field switched on and passed over the corn.

"Papa, look at the lights!"

"Shhh."

"Why?"

"Shhh."

The lights came over us and we froze. The white beams flowed on by and we moved again. The rain was like silver needles in the lights.

Water ran down my face, down inside my shirt. Dani, a gray movement just two rows over, held his hand over his eyes to block the flow. My heart pounded now–not from the walking, but from the last terror I had not told them of.

The leaves of the corn scraped by my face, rasped on my ears. Kalman fell asleep on my shoulder. It seemed incredible to me, even then in that extremity, that children could sleep anywhere.

Suddenly I was aware that Henrik was not with us.

"Stop!"

Ilona and Dani froze in mid-step. The row between Dani and me was empty. I handed Kalman to Dani.

"Stay put."

I started back through the row, looking with more than normal sight into that black and muddy world.

"Henrik!"

I ran then, beating the stalks away from me.

"Son!"

Between my gasps for air, I heard "Papa, Papa."

I went across the rows toward the sound.

"Henrik! Call to me!"

Suddenly he was ahead of me, running toward the station again. I overran him and grabbed him.

"Henrik, what are you doing?"

"Oh, Papa," he said, "I was running after you!"

I held him to me as though I would crush him. "You got turned around, son."

"I fell, Papa."

His tears were heavier than the rain.

"It's all right now. Papa found you. Papa found you."

Ilona kissed him and looked to me, but asked me nothing. We went on through the wet and rustling dead corn.

At last the corn thinned out, and we were at the edge of a great plowed field. On the other side was the wire–the flimsy, terrible border.

We crouched in the corn. They waited for me to speak. The rain drove down on us, splattering and rattling on the stalks. When the lights passed over a second time, I made my decision.

"Gab said that some borders have land mines. Some don't."

There was no answer from anyone. Finally, Ilona's voice came to me, hardly above the noise of the rain.

"How do we know?"

"We don't."

Again there was no speaking.

At last Dani said, "As God wills, I say."

"Yes," said Ilona.

I felt for their hands, one then the other.

"When I say to go, we all go together. Henrik, do you understand?"

"Yes, Papa."

Dani said, "I've got him."

The rain was pounding now. We were soaked, the water running into our shoes. The army kept the ground plowed smooth, to look for footprints, but I was sure this rain would take our secret to the streams.

I watched for the lights to pass once more.

"Now!"

We ran. The mud caked to our shoes and our legs, slowing us down. Ilona struggled, and I took her by the arm and lifted her. The lights arced on the far end of the field and started back for us. We were but seconds from the border.

"God," I cried out, "help us!"

The lights swept through again, but this time we were behind their range. We were over the wire, all of us.

I dropped to my knees in the Austrian soil, holding my sons to me, and in the pouring rain, I wept.

Epilogue

Less than two months later we landed in the United States. I stepped off the airplane with the overwhelming sense that I had been released from prison.

I told our story to an interpreter, and she cried as she told it to the officials. She turned back to me once and said, "I am so glad you have come here."

She found us a sponsor family and checked on us once a month until we were settled. I applied to a university a year later and was accepted with a full scholarship. Perhaps I will be a doctor after all.

Near Christmas the following year, I received a package from Hungary. The interpreter had forwarded it from the camp, for it had borne only a label: Zoltán Galambos, United States of America. It was Kovaly's writing.

I pulled the package open. Inside was only one thing–a tin of black shoe polish. With a pounding heart, I pressed the lid up. In the middle of the new polish were the marks of two fingers, in one quick swipe, such as a boy who had a hole in his sock might make in it, were it held out to him. I put my fingers to the marks. Bootblack was found, was safe.

The inside of the lid was scratched. I passed my thumb over the mar, and then I realized it was not a mar at all, but another message–just two words etched with a pin into the metal–of someone else safe at last forever: *Mother too.*

Author's Note

The real Zoltán Galambos, Zoltán Gaal, lived a life much like the one presented in this story, although in many ways it was more dramatic and, in some places, more grim. He and his wife Ilona are always ready to testify to the ever-present "care of our Heavenly Father."

Zoltán Gaal did not leave Hungary in 1947. He stayed nine more years, trying to right what was in his power to accomplish and trying to have hope in the plans for Hungary's independence under the new Premier, Imre Nagy. He returned to school, this time at the University of Szeged. There he distinguished himself as a scholar and a Christian, graduating with a degree in science in 1954. He taught chemistry and biology in the University after that.

By 1956, conditions in Hungary had become intolerable, and Zoltán Gaal decided to leave, his family escaping in much the same way as the characters in the book do. Because he had children with him, Zoltán was selected ahead of others to be flown to the United States.

The Gaals knew no one in the United States, but they trusted the Lord to care for them there as He had in Hungary. At Camp Kilmore, they waited for a family to volunteer to sponsor them. Zoltán held school for his children, teaching them English and reading to them from the Bible. His efforts were overheard by members of a committee from Glen Falls, New York, who were looking for men to work there.

Zoltán's diploma was transferred to the United States, and he accepted a position teaching chemistry in a high school in Valatie, near Albany, New York. Later he moved to Glen Falls and taught chemistry and other sciences in a senior high school and a junior high school in Queensbury, New York.

Now retired, Zoltán Gaal and Ilona live in Greenville, South Carolina. They have four sons, all living in the United States. Ilona's sister, Margarette, lives in the United States as well. The Gaals have had visits from other members of their families who are still living in Hungary.

When asked what advice he would give young people, Mr. Gaal says, "Because everything is so different now–the culture, the times–I cannot give any specific advice. All I say is, always be aware that when something is happening to you, God may be directing your life."

D. L. W.

Ilona and Zoltán Gaal on
the day they married

Zoltán and Ilona Gaal

Zoltán Gaal's class at Gymnásium
(Zoltán in last row, third from right; Kovaly center, second row)

Református Timótheus Árvaház   KOMÁROM.

Orphanage in Komárom, Hungary

Zoltán Gaal on
graduation day from
Gymnásium

Ilona Vrabel
(right) and friend

The Gaals on the day they became citizens of the United States